Sidetracked to Danger

Frank walked into the station just ahead of the train. The locomotive was an awesome sight— massive, black iron, chugging and puffing huge balloons of white steam into the night air.

The steam whistle blew an old-fashioned and very loud harmony—a chord of three notes.

As Frank waved to Jackson in the crowd waiting for him up ahead, he felt a hard shove in his back. He lurched forward, stumbling toward the edge of the platform.

Behind him, he heard the wheezing iron giant plowing into the station.

Frank flailed his arms wildly in the air to try to regain his balance, but he couldn't. With a jolt of terror in the pit of his stomach, he plunged off the cement platform four feet to the tracks below.

The braking squeals of the locomotive filled his ears, and he could feel the tracks vibrating beneath him. . . .

The Hardy Boys Mystery Stories

Available from MINSTREL Books

THE HARDY BOYS® MYSTERY STORIES

130

The
HARDY
BOYS®

SIDETRACKED TO DANGER

FRANKLIN W. DIXON

A MINSTREL® BOOK

PUBLISHED BY POCKET BOOKS

New York   London   Toronto   Sydney   Tokyo   Singapore

A MINSTREL PAPERBACK *Original*

 A Minstrel Book published by
POCKET BOOKS, a division of Simon & Schuster Inc.
1230 Avenue of the Americas, New York, NY 10020

Copyright © 1995 by Simon & Schuster Inc.

Front cover illustration by Vince Natale

Produced by Mega-Books, Inc.

ISBN: 0-671-87214-1

First Minstrel Books printing February 1995

10 9 8 7 6 5 4 3 2 1

THE HARDY BOYS MYSTERY STORIES is a trademark
of Simon & Schuster Inc.

THE HARDY BOYS, A MINSTREL BOOK and colophon
are registered trademarks of Simon & Schuster Inc.

Printed in the U.S.A.

Contents

SIDETRACKED TO DANGER

1 A Change of Schedule

"Come on, guys, let's move it!" Seventeen-year-old Joe Hardy grabbed his bags and jumped the three steps down from the train. He zipped his football jacket against the February chill and pulled a red-and-white striped ski hat over his blond hair.

Joe turned to wait for his older brother, Frank, and their friend, twenty-two-year-old Jackson Wyatt.

"We can't be late," Jackson said. "It took me two years to convince Hamilton Harte to let me see his prize collection of model trains—and six months to talk him into letting you guys come with me."

Jackson ran a hand through his light brown hair and stuffed his glasses into one of the sixteen pockets of his tan safari vest.

1

"Then let's go," Frank Hardy said, laughing at his friend's eagerness. A year older than his brother, and at six feet one, an inch taller, Frank had dark hair and brown eyes.

"I'll have a porter take our bags into the hotel. You get us a cab," Jackson said.

Five minutes later the three were heading west in a taxi through downtown Indianapolis, Indiana. It was Sunday night, so the traffic was light, and a cold mist filled the air.

The cab drove through an area filled with vacant lots. The only exception was a nine-story building roped off with red tape. By squinting, Frank could make out the words DO NOT CROSS THIS LINE BY ORDER OF THE INDIANAPOLIS FIRE DEPARTMENT.

Four blocks later, the taxi pulled up to a wide gate and an eight-foot-high chain-link fence. Behind the fence was a small parking lot, then a large one-story limestone building. At the far side of the parking lot sat a little building that looked like a small guardhouse. Several tall security lights shone down on the property.

Jackson paid the driver and the three friends stepped out of the cab. Frank looked around the abandoned area. "Are you sure this is it?" he asked.

Jackson checked a scrap of paper, then nodded.

"Well, now what?" Joe asked. As he spoke, a white limo pulled up, and two passengers stepped out—a short middle-aged Japanese man and a pretty teenaged girl with long black hair who looked as if she might be his daughter.

"Hello!" Jackson greeted the man. "Aren't you Yoshio Agawa? I recognize your picture from my train collectors' magazine."

"I am," the man said, "and this is my daughter, Genji." The girl smiled warmly as she extended her hand to the Hardys and Jackson.

"Agawa-san, I am honored to meet you," Jackson said with a slight nod. "These are my friends Frank and Joe Hardy." Agawa bowed to them, then shook their outstretched hands.

"Mr. Agawa is from Japan and is Asia's top model train collector," Jackson said to the Hardys.

"Are you all also here to see the renowned collection of Hamilton Harte, my chief rival?" Agawa asked.

"Yes," Frank said. "We're here for a week on winter break." As he spoke, a sleek black Ferrari drove up and the gate opened automatically. The car pulled into a parking space and a tall man stepped out. He motioned Frank and Joe and the others through the gate, and the gate swung closed.

The man's dark brown hair was slicked back smoothly over the top of his head. Frank figured he was about thirty-five.

"Good evening, everyone," the man said with a thin smile. "My uncle will be a few minutes late, but I can get us out of the cold, at least."

"I am Yoshio Agawa and this is my daughter, Genji," Agawa said. "You must be Hamilton's nephew, Lane Donovan. He has mentioned you to me on several occasions."

"Mr. Agawa, your reputation precedes you. It is an honor to meet you and your daughter," Lane Donovan said, shaking Agawa's hand.

Jackson introduced himself and the Hardys. Joe noticed Donovan's handshake was quick and he barely looked at anyone. He unlocked the door to the large limestone building and ushered the group into a small room just inside.

There were a few chairs scattered around the room. Genji, Agawa, and Jackson sat down and began talking about train collecting. Joe and Frank stood awkwardly with Donovan, who simply leaned against a wall, his arms folded across his chest. Some host, Joe thought. He glanced at his brother. Frank raised an eyebrow, then shrugged.

"Uh, I noticed a building in the next block taped off by the fire department," Frank said, breaking the silence. "What's going on over there?" he asked.

"That's the Kreek Building," Donovan answered. "One of Vincent Buonnarti's latest acquisitions." Frank noticed a sneer cross Donovan's face. "He's a developer, determined to build a huge mall in this area. He's bought up all the property around here."

4

"What about this building?" Frank asked.

"Uncle Ham is at least as stubborn as Buonnarti," Donovan said. "He refuses to sell."

"Mr. Buonnarti's probably not too happy about that," Jackson said, coming over to join them.

"Correct," Donovan said. "In fact, they hate each other. Buonnarti is demolishing the Kreek Building on Tuesday unless my uncle gets his way."

"Is he trying to stop it?" Frank asked.

"Yes," Donovan answered. "Uncle Ham has fought it on the grounds that it would damage his building and its contents. He's been in court all day, trying to get it postponed. We need time to pack up the collection."

Their conversation was ended by the sound of screeching brakes. Donovan opened the door to check, and Frank saw a black Bentley zoom through the gate. Hamilton Harte, tall and thin with thick silver hair, stepped out of the car. Frank figured Harte to be about sixty.

"Yoshio," Harte said, as he stepped through the doorway. "An important day. You will see my collection at last." The two men shook hands.

"It is my honor," Agawa said with a bow.

Harte turned to Jackson. "And you, my young friend, you made it. I'm very pleased." He nodded briefly to the Hardys when Jackson introduced them. Then, his face clouding with anger, Harte

5

turned to his nephew. "The judge wouldn't stop Buonnarti," Harte said. "The demolition is still set for Tuesday afternoon. I fired my attorney."

"Don't worry, Uncle Ham," Donovan said. "We'll all help you pack up the collection."

"We'll be glad to pitch in, Mr. Harte," Jackson offered. Frank knew his friend was itching to get near such a spectacular collection.

"Not on your life," Harte said. "If it must be done, I will do it myself." He walked to a door across the room and punched a dozen numbers into the keypad that worked the lock. He pushed open the door and ushered everyone into a hall.

"Uncle Ham doesn't trust anyone with his trains," Donovan said with a crooked smile. "Not even me."

Harte unlocked a second door that opened into a large circular room. As they stepped through the doorway, Genji gasped and Joe let out a long, low whistle. Jackson's jaw dropped as he looked around, and Agawa's eyes twinkled in appreciation.

Frank figured that the room was about forty feet in diameter. It had a high ceiling studded with small spotlights. He noticed that there were three doors—the one the group had come in through, a second that led to a workroom, and another that was closed. The third door had no knob or handle and looked to be made of metal.

6

"The collection," Harte announced proudly, gesturing toward the center of the room.

In the middle of the room was a twenty-by-ten-foot table display covered with carefully arranged trains. More of the collection was locked in lighted glass-topped tables or tall display cabinets around the walls.

Hamilton perched on a tall stool at the far end of the table and began tinkering with a switch. "Lane," he barked at his nephew. "Show them around while I prepare the demonstration."

Donovan nodded at his uncle and began pointing out items of interest to Agawa and Genji. Jackson showed Joe the display cases, occasionally letting out a gasp of admiration. Frank followed behind, pausing to look more closely at a piece here and there.

"What's this?" Joe asked, pointing to a five-car train eight inches long.

"It's a tin set that was a souvenir of the Gold Rush days in California in 1850," Jackson explained.

"And here is a Wild West pay car," Donovan added, joining the group. It looked like a miniature bank on wheels, with three teller windows on one side. "It's a model of the car that would pay off cowboys when they finished a cattle drive."

"Cool," Frank said.

As Donovan pointed out antique models that

7

operated on steam produced by alcohol lamps, Frank noticed that although Harte's nephew knew a lot about the models, he didn't seem to be very enthusiastic.

"What's his angle?" Joe whispered to his brother. "He seems pretty bored about the whole deal." Joe's words echoed Frank's thoughts.

"Yoshio, how long will you be in town?" Harte asked from his perch.

"We are staying with family friends, the Moores," Agawa said. "I am conducting business while in town, so our departure depends on that."

Harte adjusted a switch and asked, "And you boys? You're at the Union Station Hotel, I'll bet."

"Where else?" Jackson said. "I've been there before, but Frank and Joe haven't seen it yet."

"You're in for a treat," Harte said. "It was the first union station in the country."

"What's a union station?" Genji asked.

"When all the railroad lines coming into the city shared the same station, they called it a union station," Harte explained. "In 1893 there were two hundred trains running through Indianapolis every day."

"Could we please begin the demonstration, Uncle Ham?" Donovan asked with a hint of impatience in his voice. "I'm not sure everyone is as interested in real trains as you are. They came to see your models." He sat stiffly on one of the chairs that had been placed around the room.

"You're mistaken there," Jackson said. "A train nut is a train nut. If you love models, you love the big ones, and vice versa."

"That's definitely true of Jackson," Joe added. "He's even learning to drive the things."

Jackson's face lit up. "I spent last summer earning my fireman's certificate on the Bayport Iron Horse. That's a *train* fireman," he said to Genji, "the one who stokes the engine with coal and wood."

"I know, I know," Genji said. "My father's a collector, remember?"

"And you're learning to be an engineer now, right?" Frank asked his friend.

"Sure am," Jackson said. "I'm an apprentice, but I'll be certified soon. Man, I love that loco."

Harte, Agawa, and Jackson compared notes on locomotives they had ridden in and worked on while Frank, Joe, and Genji walked around the display table, looking at the fabulous collection. Donovan stayed seated, clearly bored.

"Where are you from, Genji?" Frank asked.

"Kyoto, Japan," Genji answered, "but I'm in school in London right now."

"That explains your excellent English," Frank said.

9

"Students in Japan are taught English from the first grade," Genji said. "And because of my father's business, I've spent some time in the United States. I'm on break right now, so I thought I'd join Father and visit my friends here."

Suddenly, the loud voices of Agawa and Harte interrupted them. The Hardys and Genji walked over to Jackson. "What's up?" Frank asked.

"They're arguing about the Wild West pay car," Jackson answered quietly.

"You stole that car from me," Agawa said. His black eyes seemed to be shooting sparks.

"I most certainly did not," Harte said. "I bought it fair and square."

"You couldn't have," Agawa said. "That car was offered in an international phone auction last August," Agawa said. "I placed the highest bid."

"How do you know?" Harte asked. "All bids were secret and confidential."

"The owner told me so himself," Agawa said through clenched teeth. "Then, twenty-four hours after the deadline, his attorney called to say there had been a mistake. There was a higher bid."

Joe was surprised by Agawa's vehemence. Harte didn't seem fazed by the argument. In fact, Joe thought, Harte seemed to be enjoying it.

Agawa glared at Harte. "It was you, you thief! You paid someone off to get that car after the deadline. You knew how much I wanted it." He stepped closer to the case and peered inside at the small model, then up at his rival. "I will have this car, Hamilton, I promise you that."

"Not as long as I'm alive," Harte said with a chuckle. "Now, if everyone's ready, I'm prepared to begin the formal demonstration."

The group gathered around the massive table display, and Joe could see that Agawa was still seething. From under his shirt, Harte pulled a five-inch silver whistle that hung on a leather strap around his neck. Using his fingers to play the holes on the whistle, he blew a series of tones.

The viewers gasped as the trains started up. There was so much going on, they didn't know where to look first. Track turnouts and switches sent trains through a city, complete with interurban subways and overhead elevated trains.

The trains continued into the countryside, through villages and mountains, past complex farms and a desert ghost town, over river trestles and under steel truss bridges. Standing across from Agawa, Joe could see that the man was so engrossed in the demonstration he began to calm down.

Frank walked around the end of the display to get a better view from the long side. As he leaned closer to the table, there was a loud *KA-BOOM!*

11

A series of quick, deafening blasts roared through the room. Hundreds of tiny trees and miniature buildings trembled. The floor shook, and Frank saw Joe lose his balance. The younger Hardy slammed sideways into the glass door of a tall cabinet!

2 Train Robbery!

"Joe!" Frank called, running over to his brother. Joe lay on the floor next to the display cabinet that he had slammed into and its contents—three dozen cast-iron models of the steam engines called pufferbellies. "Are you okay?" Frank asked.

Joe sat up and rubbed his arm. "I guess so," he said. "At least none of these trains were damaged."

"Was there an earthquake?" Genji asked hesitantly.

"Buonnarti!" Harte said, his voice an angry whisper.

Frank and Jackson helped Joe stand up. Then the group rushed through the hall and front room and out into the parking lot.

"Look!" Frank said, pointing ahead as they ran. It looked like a bomb had hit. The nine-story Kreek

13

Building was gone. In its place was a pile of bricks, jumbled coils of electrical wiring, and shattered pipes and plaster.

In front of the pile was a stocky man in his fifties. He wore yellow coveralls and a hard hat.

"I knew it," Harte yelled. "Vincent Buonnarti," he said to the man. "You maniac!"

"Uncle Ham," Donovan said, grabbing Harte's arm. "Don't!"

"Look carefully, old man," Buonnarti said, gesturing to the remains behind him. "One day your building will be a heap of sticks and stones just like this."

As Buonnarti laughed, Harte lunged at him. Frank and Donovan reached for Harte, but he was too quick. Although older than Buonnarti, Harte was apparently in better shape than the squat, overweight developer. He wrestled Buonnarti to the ground just as a police car drove up.

"Okay, break it up," one of the policemen said, jumping out of his car. "What's going on?"

Frank helped Donovan calm Harte down. Several fire trucks pulled up, accompanied by more police cars, a van carrying the bomb squad, and a swarm of reporters and photographers.

The fire chief burst out of one car and tore over to Buonnarti. "What happened here?" the chief asked.

"I'll tell you what happened," Harte insisted.

14

"Buonnarti blew up his building tonight instead of Tuesday when it was scheduled. Arrest him!"

"Is that true, Mr. Buonnarti?" the fire chief asked, frowning. Frank and Joe eased closer to the action, not wanting to miss anything that was said.

"It was an accident," Buonnarti said. "My shooter and I were just checking on the explosives' locations for Tuesday. We're not sure what happened. Something set off the first explosion, and the chain reaction couldn't be stopped." Frank noticed the hint of a nasty smile on Buonnarti's face.

"Liar!" Harte sputtered. "He's been harassing me for months, trying to get me to sell my property to him," he said to the officer. "This is just one more attempt to bully me into caving in. I insist that you arrest him. I'll sign a complaint."

"We're going to look into it, sir," the policeman said. "Meanwhile, I suggest you return to your building and calm down."

After giving a statement to the police, Harte, accompanied by his nephew and the Agawas, began the short walk back to his building. The Hardys and Jackson hung back a moment, hoping for some more information.

"Come to my office at ten on Tuesday," Buonnarti yelled at Harte's back. "I'm unveiling the model of my mall. See what's going up after your building comes down." Harte swung around to face Buonnarti, but Donovan restrained him.

15

Frank, Joe, and Jackson lingered long enough to hear a police detective ask Buonnarti and his shooter to come to the station the next morning to make formal statements. Firemen began checking the area as Buonnarti's guards took positions around the site.

The excitement over, the three friends caught up with the others at the entrance to Harte's building. They all returned to the display room.

The model countryside looked as if a tornado had whipped through it. Miniature buildings and trees were scattered around, and small ponds spilled over their banks.

"This is a disaster," Harte fumed. He walked into the center of the room, shaking his head and shouting, "He'll do anything to get my building." The group followed carefully to be sure they didn't step on any tumbled trains.

Jackson and Agawa reached to help place some of the fallen items back in their original positions, but Harte pushed them away.

"No!" Harte yelled. "No one touch anything!" He pointed at the door. "Everyone out. The demonstration is postponed until tomorrow. Come back at five-thirty."

Donovan ushered the group outside. "Do you think Hamilton will be ready for us tomorrow?" Agawa asked Donovan in the parking lot.

"If Uncle Ham says he'll be ready, he will," Donovan replied. "He'll stay all night if he has to."

"At least he's letting us come back," Jackson said.

"Genji, maybe you could spend some time with us tomorrow before we come over here," Joe said.

Genji looked at her father, then said, "I'd love to. I'll call you tomorrow morning and let you know."

Genji and Agawa left in the limo for the Moores'. Donovan gave the Hardys and Jackson a lift back to Union Station.

"Let me give you a quick tour," Jackson said as they entered the Station, a 75,000-square-foot building divided into three sections. Frank and Joe looked around the huge room rising seventy feet to an enormous curved stained-glass ceiling. "This is the original Grand Hall, the station waiting room. During the Civil War, 3,700 Confederate soldiers had slept on the floor here, waiting to go to a prisoner-of-war camp.

"Here is the old double train shed," Jackson continued. He led the Hardys into a mammoth three-story-high area that spanned two additional city blocks. "This half of the train shed has shops, a transportation museum, and a food court. But first, let's check out our hotel suite."

The third section of the station contained a unique hotel, built entirely inside the train shed.

17

The cavernous first-floor lobby had been fitted with a reservations desk, fountains, and elevators.

"This place is wild," Frank said.

Behind the reservations desk, large columns of hotel rooms and suites rose toward the original steel girders crisscrossing the ceiling.

After picking up their bags and room key, Jackson led Frank and Joe up a red iron spiral staircase to the second level. On one side of a wide hallway were ordinary hotel rooms. On the opposite side, sitting grandly against the wall atop a gravel bed and rails, were five restored train cars.

"Outstanding," Joe said. "Real train cars."

"What's the deal on the names?" Joe asked, reading the brass letters running across the top of each car. "Charlie Chaplin, Winston Churchill . . ."

"All the cars inside the building are named for famous people who visited Indy on a train during the glory days of the railroads," Jackson explained. "This one's ours." With a broad sweep of his arm, he gestured toward the P. T. Barnum car.

"Ours!" Joe said. "What do you mean?"

"They're hotel suites, old buddy," Jackson said, walking to the steps at the end of the car.

"Man, you've outdone yourself," Frank said.

"Awesome!" Joe exclaimed. "When you said you were treating us to a special hotel, I never figured it would be this cool."

They walked up the five metal steps to the vestibule or platform. Jackson unlocked the door, and they stepped inside their suite.

The car was divided into two areas: a sitting room with a sleep sofa, two chairs, tables, and a small desk; and another sleeping area with twin beds and full-size bath. A floor-to-ceiling curtain could be pulled the width of the car to separate the sections.

Colorful circus posters and fancy reproduction light fixtures lined one wall, reminding the occupants of the car's namesake.

The four large windows on the front wall of the train car had been left intact. Old-fashioned horizontal wooden window blinds opened to a view of the tiled walkway along the hall.

They unpacked, and after a meal of snacks from their train trip and conversation about Harte's collection, they decided to make an early night of it and turn in. The Hardys shared the bedroom, and Jackson slept on the sofa, which opened into a comfortable bed.

At six-thirty the next morning, the Hardys and Jackson were jolted awake by a thundering noise. "Now that *did* sound like an earthquake," Joe said. He and Frank jumped out of bed.

"I'll call the desk to make sure," Jackson said, stumbling from the sofa bed to the desk, "but I think I know what it is."

He hung up the phone. "I was right," he reported. "The Hoosier State just pulled in on Track Seven, right outside our car. It's a passenger train that rolls in every morning at six-thirty on its way to Chicago."

"This is the craziest hotel I've ever been in," Frank mumbled, while the roaring 3,000-horse-power diesel engine idled a few yards away.

Genji called at nine A.M. By that time the guys were up, dressed in jeans and sweaters, and enjoying breakfast from the hotel bakery.

"I can come any time," Genji said. "My father is busy all day. He'll meet us at Mr. Harte's."

"Great," Joe said. "Come early and check out the accommodations."

Genji was there within an hour. "Wow," she said when she saw the P. T. Barnum train car suite. "Mr. Harte was right. This place is incredible."

The four set out to explore the Station. Skylights above the train car suites flooded the hall with sunshine. A door at the end of the hall opened into the station's food court in the middle section of the train shed.

Bright with colorful banners, the food court was ringed with ethnic food shops. The center of the huge area held tables and chairs and a small stage, where a local rock group was setting up.

Jackson led the group down the escalator to the first-level shops and boutiques. After poking around the shops for a while, they checked out the transportation museum, then went back up to catch the rock show and grab lunch in the food court.

At five-fifteen they left the station and walked the few blocks past the hulking Hoosier Dome football stadium to Harte's building.

Agawa's limo was already there, and soon Harte pulled his Bentley into the parking lot. He parked it next to a rusted-out red Mustang, and he and Donovan got out. Harte nodded a few greetings and led them into the building.

Harte unlocked the first door and ushered everyone into the hall. "I was here all night," he said, "but it was worth it, gentlemen and lady." He bowed to Genji. "I am proud to demonstrate for you the finest model train collection in all the world."

"Perhaps," Agawa said, just loud enough for Joe to hear.

Harte punched in the lock combination, turned to give his visitors a last confident look, and opened the door with a dramatic flourish.

"No!" Harte said, his voice a harsh whisper. "It can't be!" Frank and Joe stepped into the room behind the collector. Stunned, they looked around.

Every table and every shelf was empty. Hamilton Harte's entire collection was gone!

3 Payback Time

"Uncle Ham!" Donovan yelled. "What happened? Where are your trains!"

The entire group looked around the room in disbelief. Everything was gone. Even the tracks were missing.

Frank scanned the floor under the table and around the cabinets. Jackson and Joe followed Harte, who raced into the workshop room. Agawa and Genji stood in the doorway with Donovan, their mouths open in astonishment.

"Everybody out!" Harte thundered, returning to the main room. "Now!" He pushed them to the door, then into the hall, and closed and locked the door.

In a few minutes, the group heard some shrill

sounds from behind the closed door. Frank recognized them as tones from the silver whistle, but he thought it was a different pattern than the one Harte had used the night before to start the trains.

By pressing next to the door, Frank and Joe could hear noises from the other side—an odd hum and a strange swishing sound.

Finally, after a twenty-minute wait, Harte unlocked and opened the display-room door and ushered the group back in from the hall.

"Lane!" Harte barked. "Get Sam Bellamy in here. I'm sure he's in the bungalow."

Donovan pushed a button on the wall phone, said a few words into the mouthpiece, and hung up. Within minutes, a short man with curly blond hair and a protruding belly entered the room. Frank figured he was about forty-five.

As he looked around the room, the man's eyes grew wider and his jaw dropped lower. "Oh no!" he said. "What happened!"

"I've been robbed, Sam," Harte's voice thundered. "Did you see or hear anything today?"

Genji joined Joe as he lingered near Harte, Donovan, and Bellamy. Frank and Jackson quietly searched the room for clues.

"No . . . no," Sam muttered. "Nothing."

"Did you leave the bungalow today?" Harte asked.

"No!" Bellamy answered. Joe noticed that the man was very nervous and agitated. He kept glancing at Donovan, then shaking his head.

As Joe watched, Agawa moved casually over to Harte. "When did you leave the building, Hamilton?" Agawa asked.

"Why ask, Yoshio?" Donovan said, his mouth twisted in a sneer. "Maybe you already know!"

Joe heard Genji gasp in surprise. Frank and Jackson walked over to join Joe and Genji. They could see that Harte was becoming more agitated.

"Lane's right," Harte said. Maybe you know because you were watching, and as soon as I left, you came in here and—"

"Hamilton, be reasonable," Agawa said. "You are extremely upset by what has happened, but you have gone too far. Although we have had our skirmishes in the past, you know I wouldn't do such a thing."

Frank took a bold step forward. "When *did* you leave the building, Mr. Harte?" he asked.

"The repairs went well until I got to the telltale," Harte said, slumping into a chair. "I ran out of parts but knew I had some at home. Sam was on duty when I left."

"He returned to our home about six this morning," Donovan added. "I fixed him some tea before I left for a meeting."

"Unfortunately, it was a mistake to work all

24

night," Harte said. "After I found the parts I needed and repaired the telltale, I was too tired to come back down here. I called Sam. He usually is on duty until nine A.M. but I asked him to stay on until this afternoon."

"And I did," Sam said. "The electronic security was on, of course. Didn't want to take any chances, what with that nut blowing up buildings."

"An electronic security system?" Joe said.

"Yes, and it is very sophisticated. It will keep anyone from getting in," Harte said. "Sam's job is to keep people out of the parking lot and away from the building."

"They were obviously professional thieves," Donovan said. "They know all about how to get around security systems nowadays."

"Mr. Harte, I—I—" Bellamy stammered.

"Get out, Sam," Harte said, waving his hand. "Whoever did it strolled right past your window."

"He should stay to talk to the police," Frank said, joining the group. "They'll have questions."

Harte looked at Frank as if he was seeing him for the first time. Frank saw an odd look come over Harte's face.

"Absolutely not," Harte said. A new determination seemed to surge through him. He squared his shoulders and jumped to his feet.

"My friend is correct," Agawa said firmly. "There is no need to involve the authorities at this time. This may be a matter that can be settled privately. Police can be called later if necessary.''

"Father, I don't get it," Genji asked. "What do you mean, 'settled privately'?"

"It's likely my trains were kidnapped and will be ransomed," Harte said. "If so, I should hear soon. If not, there is only one answer: That warthog Buonnarti is behind it. One more attempt to get me to cave in to his demands to sell."

The Hardys watched in surprise as anger turned Harte's face dark red. "And he'll pay dearly."

"Hamilton, I suggest you enlist everyone's cooperation in keeping this quiet from the police and the press," Agawa urged.

"Yes," Donovan agreed. "Everyone here must pledge secrecy about the events that have taken place in this building over the last twenty-four hours. Is that clear? Do not tell *anyone*."

Each of the group nodded and murmured consent to Harte's demand. Shortly after that, the Hardys and Jackson left. They walked the few blocks to their hotel, stopping in the food court to grab some sandwiches and soda to go.

Back in the Barnum car, Frank and Joe were revved up by the evening's turn of events. "Looks like we have a case," Joe said, grinning.

Jackson was quiet. "It's terrible," he finally said. "It's every collector's nightmare."

26

"So, do we think the trains really were stolen?" Joe asked around a huge bite of his thick sandwich.

"What do you mean?" Frank asked.

"Well, it's pretty fishy that Harte doesn't want to report it to the police," Joe said. "Maybe he needs money and stashed the trains himself. Plans to cash in on a big insurance payoff."

"Then that makes Agawa a suspect, too," Frank said. "He was also firm about not calling the police. I wonder what he meant when he said he and Harte had had their skirmishes in the past."

"Well, they're pretty fierce rivals, I'll bet," Jackson said. "I'll try to find out more about that— maybe at the local collectors' club."

"Not Genji's dad," Joe groaned. "That'd be such a rotten deal for her."

"How about that guard, Bellamy?" Jackson said.

"I tell you, he was pretty nervous when they were questioning him," Frank said.

"You'd be nervous, too, if a million dollars' worth of trains were stolen right under your nose," Jackson said, stashing the remains of his supper in the small refrigerator in the corner.

"Where'd Harte get all his money, anyway?" Joe asked. "That collection was amazing."

"Railroading, of course," Jackson answered. "His family owned half the railroads in the Midwest. And that was back when railroads were the only

27

way to travel and move freight. Most of them are out of business now, but he made his bucks first."

"Who do *you* think stole the collection?" Joe asked. "Professional thieves, like Donovan said?"

"I don't know," Jackson answered. "It might be tough to sell to collectors. Besides, it's pretty hard to swallow Vincent Buonnarti's story about the demolition. The accidental explosion story is mighty suspicious."

"Sure is," Frank agreed. "It might have been another harassment scheme to drive Harte out of his building. In fact, I'm going to check out Buonnarti tomorrow morning. Who's with me?"

"I am," Joe said. "You know I can't resist a mystery. Where do we go first?"

"Buonnarti's unveiling the scale model of his mall tomorrow," Frank said.

"Perfect," Joe said, taking a final swig of his soda and sailing the can expertly into the wastebasket.

"Why don't you head over there and check it out," Frank said. "I'll go to the newspaper office first. I want to check the archives, see what's been going on with this land grab Buonnarti launched. I'll meet you for the unveiling."

"You guys are on your own," Jackson said. "The local model train club holds their weekly meeting tomorrow. I don't want to miss it."

"Great," Frank said. "Ask around there. See if you can find out anything about Agawa. By the way, what's a telltale?" Frank asked. "Harte said he had to go home to repair his telltale."

Jackson pulled a paper and pencil from one of his vest pockets and drew the Hardys a picture. "It's a wooden pole with a crossarm that extends out over the track," he said, drawing an upside-down L.

"A dozen ropes hang down from it." He drew twelve lines straight down that looked like fringe from the top of the upside-down L. "These were placed alongside the trackbed before the entrances to tunnels and low bridges. The ropes hung over the trains."

"Why?" Joe asked.

"Originally, trains were braked mechanically. A brakeman had to climb onto the roof of every car and manually turn a wheel to set the brakes. Then he'd jump to the next car and turn the wheel to work that brake and so on through all the cars.

"I think that qualifies for hazardous duty," Joe said, with a low whistle.

"Especially if the train was headed toward a tunnel or low bridge and he had his back to it," Jackson pointed out.

"Ah, the telltale." Frank nodded.

"If the brakeman was on the roof and felt the ropes of a telltale on the back of his neck and head, he knew it meant 'Duck! Fast!'"

"I get it," Joe said. "The brakeman would drop and flatten himself on the roof so his head wouldn't

29

be knocked off when the train pulled into the tunnel, right?"

"You got it," Jackson said.

"I wish Harte's display room could tell a few tales," Frank said. "Like who stole the collection, for one. And why."

"Looks like it's up to us to find that out," Joe said.

The next morning the group split up. Jackson went to the collectors' meeting across town, Frank to the newspaper office downtown, and Joe to Buonnarti corporate headquarters.

Buonnarti had a complex of three buildings spaced around a well-landscaped city block. Joe headed for the press room of the main building with a group of reporters, city bigwigs, and interested citizens. A large table covered with a cloth stood in the center of the room.

At ten, Buonnarti walked in and took his place at the speaker's stand in the front of the room. As he adjusted the mike, Frank slipped in next to Joe.

"I got a bunch of stuff," Frank whispered. He pulled some photocopies of newspaper articles out of a large envelope.

"Buonnarti tried lots of things to get Harte to knuckle under," he told Joe. "He even tried to get the city to declare eminent domain—take over the building for public use. They were all legal schemes, but they were all denied."

"Sounds like he might be a little frustrated," Joe said quietly, not wanting anyone to hear him. "Maybe he's decided to try some not-so-legal ideas." He saw his brother's forehead wrinkle. "What are you looking at?"

"That man over there—the one with the red hair and the Indianapolis Colts cap," Frank answered. "I'm sure I just saw him at the newspaper archives."

"Hmm," Joe said, watching the stranger. "Maybe he's following the same trail we are."

"Welcome, ladies and gentlemen," boomed the voice from the microphone. "My name is Vincent Buonnarti."

"And you are a crook!" The crowd was electrified by the sudden shouting from the rear of the room. The Hardys recognized the voice of Hamilton Harte. He stood inside the door, a dark green duffel bag slung over his shoulder.

"Security!" Buonnarti cried. "Call security!"

"You are a thief and an extortionist, Buonnarti," Harte declared through clenched teeth. "And it's payback time." Before Frank or Joe could move, Harte reached into his duffel bag and whipped out a huge, glistening machete!

4 Another Suspect

The room erupted into noise and action as Hamilton swung the machete. Chairs crashed to the floor as people raced for the nearest exit. A couple of people screamed for help.

"Call security!" Buonnarti yelled. "Call the police!" He pounded on the podium.

The reporters and photographers who had gathered for the model unveiling went to work, jotting notes and snapping pictures.

Frank approached Harte. "Mr. Harte, you don't want to do anything you'll regret," he said as calmly as he could. "Put down the machete and let's talk."

Harte wouldn't be stopped. With long determined strides, he charged toward the table in the middle of the room and whipped off the cloth.

The mall model glistened with snowy white

paint. The machete whistled through the air once, twice, three times. Within seconds, the model was a heap of wood scraps.

Just then, two policemen and a security guard burst into the room. They grabbed the machete and restrained Harte by pulling his arms behind him.

"My mall!" Buonnarti yelled. He jumped off the stage and ran to his ruined display. "Look what you did." He glared at Harte with such hatred that a policeman pulled Harte back farther, out of range of Buonnarti's beefy arms and clenched fists.

"I was going to surprise you with this, but I'll enjoy telling you now," Buonnarti said to Harte. "I am asking the city to open the downtown underground rooms." His lips curled into a nasty smirk. "There'll be restaurants and shops in my mall. Pretty soon I'll own not only everything around your building, but everything under it as well."

Joe was startled by Harte's reaction. For a moment, the blood seemed to drain from the man's face, and his eyes bulged as they grew wider. His expression was not anger—it was panic. Joe quickly glanced at his brother, who was staring at Harte. Obviously Frank noticed the odd reaction, too.

Then Harte's rage returned with more energy than before, and he tried to break free of the policeman's hold. Buonnarti stormed out of the room, and Joe was relieved to see Lane Donovan rush into the room. Maybe he can calm his uncle down, Joe thought. On seeing his nephew, Harte seemed finally to relax.

"What happened?" Donovan asked. "Uncle Ham! What's going on?" The Hardys filled him in on what had happened.

"Mr. Donovan," Frank continued, "we will be happy to help in any way."

"Thank you," Donovan said. "I can handle it. This really is a private matter."

"What's going to happen to him?" Frank asked one of the policemen. "Where are you taking him?"

"We're taking him in to cool off a little," the policeman said. "After that, it's up to Buonnarti." The policeman escorted Harte out, with Donovan following.

Suddenly, a reporter was directly in Joe's path.

"Who are you and what do you know about what happened here?" the reporter demanded.

"Uh, nothing for the record," Joe answered, trying to get by.

"Come on," Frank said, "let's get out of here." They headed on foot back toward Monument Circle. Frank turned to see if they were being followed, and they were—but not by the press.

"Don't look back, but we've got company," Frank said, turning around. "It's the guy with the red hair and Colts cap who I pointed out to you—the same one I saw at the newspaper office. I think he's following us."

34

"Let's surprise him," Joe said, rubbing his hands together. They slowed their pace until they heard the man about half a block back. Then, at Joe's signal, they turned at once to confront him.

Startled, the stranger hesitated, then bolted. He ran across the street and down an alley. Frank and Joe followed him to the entrance to Union Station. A group of tourists plunging through the door forced the Hardys back, and by the time they entered the station, the man was gone.

Frank and Joe darted through the first floor, checking the shops and the small arched nooks throughout the grand hall, but there was no trace of the red-haired stranger.

They tore up the stairs to the food court, but their quarry had disappeared into the crowd. "Rats," Frank said, "we've lost him."

"What's our next move?" Joe asked.

"As long as we're here, we might as well grab some lunch," Frank said, checking his watch. "You pick up something. I'll find us a table."

Frank sat down at a small table in the center of the room and pulled out the articles he had photocopied from the newspaper office.

When Joe returned with two burritos and two sodas, Frank showed him an article. "Look at this," Frank said. "It's about Buonnarti's plans. It mentions the 'underground.' There are rooms under the City Market and under a place called Silvio's Diner—"

"That's just a few blocks from here," Joe said. "We passed it coming back from Harte's building last night."

Frank nodded, then continued reading. "And rumors of rooms beneath Union Station."

"Whoa," Joe said, looking at the paper. "Cool."

"Remember the look that Harte gave Buonnarti when the developer said he was going to use the underground as part of his mall?" Frank asked.

"How could I forget," Joe said. "It was half fury, half panic. The news really got to him." Joe fiddled with his straw for a minute. "You know," he said thoughtfully, "Silvio's is really close to Harte's. If Buonnarti uses the rooms under Silvio's for the mall, the development could go right under Harte's building."

"Maybe there's something in the underground that Harte doesn't want anyone to know about," Frank suggested. He took a bite of his burrito. "Looks as if we have some exploring to do, bro."

When they finished eating, they walked downstairs to the grand hall again. Frank noticed an old man retouching the paint on an ornate carved arch. "Hi," Frank said. "How's it going?"

"Just fine," the painter said.

"I'll bet you're kept pretty busy around here," Frank said.

36

"Busy enough," the man answered. "Been working steady since the restoration began in 1986."

"I hear there are rooms underground beneath the station," Frank said. "Have you been down there?"

"Nope," the man said. "They've been closed a long time—can't get to them now." He stepped back to check his work. "Nobody I know's ever seen them. May just be a rumor."

"How about that new mall that's going up around here?" Joe asked. "Maybe those rooms could be used for stores in the mall."

"Some of the underground could be used, I guess," the old gentleman said. "The rooms under Silvio's might work. You got enough money, anything can be done, I suppose."

Frank and Joe thanked the man and went through the doors to the hotel side. When they reached the lobby, Jackson and Agawa were just coming in the hotel's front door.

"Mr. Agawa was at the collectors' meeting," Jackson said. "He offered his car to bring me back here."

"I would be pleased if you all would join me for lunch," Agawa said.

"Well, we've already—" Joe began, but he stopped when Frank shot him a look.

"Thank you, sir," Frank said, smiling. "We'd love to."

The four found a table at an Italian restaurant in

the station. After they ordered, Jackson said, "I tell you, this is really an exciting week for me, Agawa-san. To be spending time with both you and Hamilton Harte is a dream come true."

Agawa smiled and turned to the Hardys. "And you two," he said. "Are you collectors also?"

"No, just fans," Frank said.

"Jackson brought us along for the ride," Joe said. "The theft is a real drag."

"Yes, a tragedy to have such a collection stolen," Agawa murmured. He looked away and seemed to be lost in his own thoughts.

"Frank and Joe are old friends of mine," Jackson said. "I had read about a case they solved involving computer fraud. I was so interested I looked them up."

Joe laughed. "We meet a lot of people that way."

"'Solved'?" Agawa said. Frank noticed that Genji's father snapped out of his silent thoughts immediately. His eyes gleamed.

"How do you mean, 'solved'?" he said. "Are you two computer wizards?"

"Agawa-san's company designs computer chips," Jackson explained, digging into his salad. "No, sir," he said with a laugh, "they're not hackers. They're detectives. It runs in their family—their dad is one, too."

"Detectives!" Agawa said. He seemed genuinely

38

startled. "Why, I'm . . . I'm surprised to hear that. . . . I had no idea."

"It's no big deal," Frank said hastily. He should have warned Jackson not to blow their cover. After all, Agawa could be one of their suspects.

Agawa looked at his watch, then said, "I'm afraid I must leave you now. I just remembered a very important call that I must make. I will take care of the bill on my way out. Please, stay and enjoy yourselves." He stood, bowed slightly, and was gone before any of them could say goodbye.

"Busy man," Jackson said.

"I wonder if that's all it is," Frank replied. "He left kind of abruptly."

"I agree," Joe said. "Well, come on, Jackson, old boy, eat up. Frank and I have had two lunches today already. How about a lap or two around the plaza?"

Within minutes, the three were outside on the red bricks of the station's plaza. The afternoon had warmed in the sun. A crowd had gathered around a street entertainer who was juggling bowling balls. Sidewalk vendors sold hot dogs, pretzels, and peanuts from their carts.

Joe stepped onto the brick plaza, heading toward the juggler. He had taken only a few steps when he heard a sound.

It was loud, a wild, clattering noise. Joe turned and his heart leapt into his throat. A huge, snorting horse, its mouth foaming with lather, had jumped the curb and was headed toward the crowd. It pulled an empty white wobbling carriage behind it.

Joe yelled and ran toward the runway. Then he felt his ankle wrench and he tripped, landing hard on the bricks.

He looked up to see the horse turn, sweat flying from its massive tan neck. His heart pounding, Joe scrambled backward on the bricks, trying to regain his footing.

The horse turned again. Joe could see the fiery panic in the animal's eyes as it headed straight for him!

5 To Market, to Market

"Joe!" Frank shouted. He rushed to the horse and carriage, grabbed the dangling reins, and yanked hard. The horse had so much momentum that it dragged him a few yards over the brick plaza.

"Whoa! Whoa! Easy, boy!" Frank yelled. Finally, the weight of Frank's body broke the steed's gallop, and the lumbering horse stumbled to a stop two feet in front of Joe.

People gathered around, and a policeman helped Joe to his feet. Within minutes, the carriage driver limped up to claim the horse and carriage.

"What happened?" the policeman asked.

"I'm not sure," the driver said. "I was parked there." He pointed across the street. "I was on the sidewalk folding a lap robe, and someone flew by me and smacked Ranger hard on the rump."

The driver pointed to the horse's flank. "Look. He must have used a two-by-four."

"'He'?" The policeman repeated, jotting notes.

"I think so," the driver answered. "It all happened so fast. Ranger reared up and bolted before I could grab the reins."

"Did you see the man?" Joe asked.

"Yeah, he was wearing a Colts cap," the driver said. "But I couldn't see his face."

"Too bad," the policeman said, shaking his head. The horse snorted and shivered as the driver patted its neck. "If you can think of anything, even a tiny detail, give us a call."

The driver led the horse from the plaza and back into the street. "I'll bet it was our red-haired guy, Joe," Frank said.

That evening, Frank, Joe, and Jackson met Genji at the RibRack, a local hangout near the station. Over burgers and fries, the Hardys told the other two about their dangerous adventures that day.

"What made you suspicious of the red-haired guy in the first place?" Genji asked, her eyes wide. "Most people probably wouldn't have noticed him."

Frank and Joe smiled, and Jackson jumped in to answer the pretty teenager. "Allow me to reintroduce my friends," he said, with a sweeping gesture.

"Frank and Joe Hardy, premier detectives of Bayport and assorted other haunts."

"No kidding?" Genji said. "Tell me more."

The Hardys and Jackson told Genji about some of Frank and Joe's experiences. "So do you think Buonnarti stole Mr. Harte's trains?" she asked.

"We don't know yet." Frank shrugged.

"Maybe I can help," Genji said eagerly. "You know we're staying with friends while we're here." She shoved her plate aside and leaned closer. "Well, last night, my father asked them about Buonnarti."

"Really?" Joe said.

"A lot of people in Indy think he's rotten," Genji said. "He's been accused of unscrupulous business practices several times. Each time he's wriggled out of trouble, but most people think he'd resort to anything to get what he wants."

"Harte sure thinks so," Jackson said, looking around the room. Several couples were dancing on the small wooden floor in the center. "The deejay here has cool taste," he said.

Genji nodded. "I love this song," she said. As she spoke, a young man asked her to dance. The pair joined the mob in the middle of the room.

"I'm glad she's out of earshot," Jackson said. "I did some snooping of my own at the train collectors' meeting, and I can't wait to tell you about it."

"So give," Frank urged.

"The competition between Harte and Agawa is really fierce," Jackson said. He reached into one of his vest pockets and took out a small notebook.

"Everyone had a story or two about how those two guys have duped each other in order to buy a valuable item," Jackson said, checking his notes.

"Are their collections equal?" Frank asked.

"Agawa has the best collection in Asia, Harte the best in North America. Overall, I'd say Harte's is better."

"So Agawa might have a motive to rip him off," Frank said.

"I wonder if Genji knows that," Joe said.

Just then, Genji returned to the table. "So what's next?" she asked as she sat down. "I'm signing on as a rookie detective. Where do we go from here?"

The three guys exchanged looks. Joe wondered if there was a way to include Genji in the investigation and also keep their suspicions about Agawa under wraps. It didn't look as if they had much choice.

"We've got to get inside Hart's building and find out how the trains were stolen," Joe said.

"We know it was sometime between six in the morning when Harte left and five-thirty in the evening when we all showed up," Jackson said.

"Right," Frank said. "You know, there's something funny about the whole theft. Harte's sup-

44

posed to have a world-class security system, plus Sam Bellamy sitting there next door."

"I agree, Frank," Genji said. "Whoever did it would have had to know Bellamy's schedule and how to trip Harte's security."

"Of course, there's one obvious person who fits that description," Frank said.

"Sam Bellamy," Joe said.

"You got it." Frank nodded. "Let's go over to Harte's building tomorrow. Maybe talk to Bellamy and see if we can come up with anything."

The four left the RibRack, agreeing to meet at the station doughnut shop the next morning at nine. Genji headed back to the Moores, and the Hardys and Jackson turned in for some much-needed sleep.

"I have something to report," Genji said excitedly as Frank, Joe, and Jackson met her outside the doughnut shop the next morning.

"Already?" Joe said. "Not bad for a rookie."

Genji grinned. "My father called Lane Donovan last night. Harte got out on bail yesterday afternoon. Donovan told my father that Harte really believes the collection was taken for ransom and that he'll be contacted soon with a demand," she said.

"Makes sense," Jackson commented.

"Professional thieves would have heard of his collection," Genji continued.

"And they'd probably know how rich he is," Joe added.

"Plus you'd have to be either crazy or desperate to try to sell it, unless you had a network of fences," Jackson pointed out. "Any sudden dumping on the market of a collection of this size would be a tipoff to the authorities immediately."

"But Harte has another idea," Genji said. "He thinks the collection might have been stolen by someone with a different kind of deal in mind."

"Buonnarti?" Frank guessed.

"Exactly!" Genji said. "Harte thinks Buonnarti engineered the theft so he can use the collection to make a deal for Harte's building. Harte tried to get Buonnarti arrested for the explosion, but the police investigation showed no evidence of anything but an accident."

"What does Donovan think?" Joe asked her as they ducked into the doughnut shop.

"Hard to say," she answered. "Mostly he wants to keep his uncle calm and the cops out of the picture."

"What's his story, anyway?" Frank asked.

"Well, according to the Moores, Donovan's parents died when he was a kid, and Harte was his only relative. Donovan was shipped around to military schools as he grew up, then just moved in to work for his uncle when he graduated. He's been there ever since."

46

"What does he do, exactly?" Frank asked.

"No one seems to know," Genji said. "Most people think he doesn't really work, that Donovan not only lives *with* his uncle, he lives *off* him."

The four friends finished their doughnuts and set out for Harte's building.

"By the way," Genji said, "I didn't tell my father exactly what we are doing today."

Joe and Frank exchanged looks. "Why not?" Joe asked. Could she have suspicions, too?

"I don't think he'd want me prowling around Harte's building," Genji explained. "Father has been acting so strange since the robbery. It really made him nervous, of course, being a collector himself." Or he could be nervous for other reasons, Joe thought.

"What's your dad doing today, Genji?" Frank tried to make the question sound like casual curiosity, not a detective's grilling.

"He's staying in today," Genji replied. "He said he's going to call some of his contacts and see if anyone's been offering any prize pieces over the last twenty-four hours."

The area around Harte's building was quiet. Frank pushed the buzzer at the fence. Bellamy came out of his bungalow and over to the gate.

Frank smiled broadly at the guard. "Hi," he said. "Frank Hardy from Monday night, remember?" He gestured one by one toward the others. "My brother, Joe; Yoshio Agawa's daughter, Genji; and Mr. Harte's friend, Jackson Wyatt."

"I remember you," Bellamy said.

"We stopped by to see Mr. Harte," Frank said.

"He's not here," Bellamy said crisply.

Joe stepped up to the gate. "It was really my idea to come here," he said quickly. "It's that Mustang." Everyone followed Joe's gaze to the rusted-out red car sitting in the parking lot. "I noticed it the other evening. Whose is it?"

"Mine," Bellamy said.

"No kidding," Joe said. "Why, it's almost a classic. You ever think of having it restored?" The others held their breath, hoping Bellamy would buy Joe's story.

Bellamy looked at the younger Hardy. Joe felt like the guard's eyes drilled right into his brain to see if he was telling the truth.

Bellamy took a deep breath and seemed to relax a little. "Nope," he said. "Never thought restoring that clunker would be worth it."

"We'd love to see it up close. C'mon," Joe urged, "let us in. I know about restoration. You could get a bundle if it were fixed up."

A glint sparkled in Bellamy's eyes and he tripped the lock and pulled the gate open. "You know something about Mustangs?" he asked as he walked over to the car with Joe.

While Joe began rattling off everything he knew

48

about Mustangs and restorations, Frank, Jackson, and Genji snooped around the car for clues.

Frank poked his head inside one of the car's windows. A jumble of paper covered the front seat—receipts, unopened bills, racetrack tout sheets.

"There's a receipt there on the dashboard," Frank said, trying to look casual. "It's from a cookie shop in the station, dated eleven A.M. Monday— the day of the robbery."

"Hey," said Genji in a low voice. "I thought he said he was on duty all that day. If he was buying cookies then, he couldn't have been here!"

"Bingo!" Frank said with a smile.

"Someone wrote a note at the bottom," Jackson whispered, peering in through the window. "I'll copy it." He reached into one of his dozen vest pockets and took out pencil and paper.

Frank brushed a twig off Bellamy's car. "Boy, that robbery was really something, wasn't it?" he said to the guard. "It must have taken a while to get all that out of there, don't you think?"

"I expect so," Bellamy said. He and Joe were bent over, inspecting the grille of his car.

"And you were here all day," Frank said.

Bellamy straightened back up and looked at Frank. "Yes, I was—the whole day," he said firmly.

"And yet you never saw or heard anything," Frank said. "The thieves were pretty slick."

Bellamy walked over and stood in front of Frank. He was so close, Frank could smell peanuts on his breath. "I was here," the guard said. "All day. I saw nothing. I heard nothing."

Neither Frank nor Bellamy moved for a minute. Finally, Joe said, "Well, thanks again for letting me check out your car. We'll come back again when Mr. Harte is going to be here."

The Hardys, Jackson, and Genji left the small parking lot and headed back to the station. Frank looked back once. Bellamy was still watching them.

Frank filled Joe in on the receipt they had seen and what it meant. "What did the note say on the bottom of the receipt, Jackson?" Frank asked.

"It said 'JPS, 7P,' and today's date," Jackson said.

"What does that mean?" Genji asked.

"Could mean a time," Frank said. "The '7P' might be seven P.M."

Jackson nodded. "Yeah, but who or what is 'JPS'?"

As soon as they got to the station, they headed for the cookie shop listed on the receipt in Bellamy's car. Frank described Sam Bellamy to the clerk and asked her if she remembered him.

"You mean this guy?" she asked. She handed him a recent clipping from the newspaper. It told about a new Thoroughbred racetrack opening ninety miles away near Louisville, Kentucky. The accompanying photo showed Bellamy as the first person through the track gates. Frank noticed that sixth in line was Lane Donovan.

"Sure," she said, with a bright smile. "He's a regular—buys a dozen chocolate chunk cookies and a large coffee every morning at eleven."

"And you're sure he was here yesterday?" Frank asked.

"You bet," the clerk said. "In fact, that's when he gave me that clipping. Look, he autographed it. Even put the date." She pointed to a sloppy scrawl.

She looked at the Hardys and their friends, then tilted her head. "Say, what's this all about?"

"We're cooking up a surprise for him," Joe said, "so don't mention that we were here, okay?"

The four investigators went upstairs to the food court for a quick lunch. "Well, that cinches it," Jackson said, his voice excited. "Sam Bellamy lied when he said he was on duty the whole day."

"There's something interesting about that photo," Joe said. "It looks like Donovan and Bellamy have the same hobby."

"After lunch, let's split up," Frank said. "Joe, you and Genji go to City Market. See if you can get more details about the underground rooms there. Jackson and I will go to Silvio's Diner and check out the rooms under there."

"Good idea," Joe said. "Harte really panicked when Buonnarti mentioned the underground."

Joe and Genji left for City Market, several blocks north of the station.

An Indy landmark, the Market had been on the same site in some form since 1832. Across the street was the city courthouse and jail, and to the east was Market Square Arena.

Joe and Genji walked across the Market's courtyard and into the large restored building. Small delis and restaurants looked down from the balcony onto bread, vegetable, and fruit stands.

"Who would know the most about this place?" Joe wondered.

"I bet he would," Genji said, pointing out a white-haired man sitting in a rocking chair in the corner of a small room along the outside wall.

Joe and Genji struck up a conversation with the man. The shelves and counters were full of Greek and Middle Eastern foods. "I've been here fifty years," the old man said, answering Joe's question.

"Is it true there are rooms below the market?" Joe said.

"Ah yes, but they aren't used anymore—too dangerous," he said. "There was a meeting hall here and rooms below called the Catacombs—rooms for dances, small meeting rooms, even a pistol range."

"What happened to them?" Genji asked, taking the apple that the old man offered her.

"The meeting hall burned, and people forgot

about the Catacombs," he said. "By the time they decided to build over them, the underground rooms were useless—rotting wood, moldy walls. Boarded up now."

Joe and Genji thanked the man and walked around until they came to a large fish market angled into a corner of the building. Joe spotted an entrance to a dark hallway behind the counter. A sign read DO NOT ENTER.

Joe waited until the salesgirl had a customer at the far end of the counter. Then he signaled to Genji and they darted behind the counter.

The hall was long and dark, with one dim light bulb hanging from the ceiling. Joe and Genji crept along the wall until it stopped at a dead end. Ahead of them was a boarded-up wall with another sign, warning, DANGER—NO ADMITTANCE.

Genji pried at a few boards with her hands. Before Joe could stop her, she had dropped down, pulled the boards out, and darted through the opening.

"Genji!" Joe called. "Don't go in there!" He squatted down and peered into the dark beyond.

Before he could get his eyes focused, three frightening sounds traveled through the darkness. First, the sharp crack of splintering wood. Then, Genji's terrified voice. Finally, a sickening thud.

6 Marching with JPS

"Genji, Genji!" Joe called into the blackness. "Answer me. Are you all right?"

"Joe!" Genji cried. "Help me."

Joe pulled a flashlight from his backpack. The sharp smell of an old basement drifted up from the darkness. Peering through the small opening at the bottom of the wall, he tried to see what had happened to Genji.

The flashlight beam showed wide stone steps leading down into what seemed to be a huge room with plaques and banners along the far wall. "Genji!" Joe called again. "Where are you?" Joe's hands were clammy with cold sweat as he panned the flashlight around.

Finally, the light caught her. She was trapped a few yards out from the bottom of the steps. "I fell through the floor," she said, with a weak smile. "The wood wouldn't hold me."

Joe pulled back out of the opening and looked around. He spotted a large T-shaped broom down the hall. "Hang in there," he said. "I'll be right back."

Joe laid the flashlight on the floor in front of the opening so Genji would have light. Then he ran to get the broom.

Grabbing the flashlight, he squirmed through the opening, breaking another board as he dragged the broom through after him. Cautiously, he walked down the six stone steps to the decaying wood floor.

He crouched on the bottom step and eased the broom across the splintered wood toward Genji. "Wrap your arms around the crossbar of the broom," he told her.

Genji did as Joe instructed. Carefully, Joe began easing the broom back. Inch by inch, he pulled, hoisting her up and out of the rotten wood. Her legs trailed out behind her. As Joe pulled her slowly across the floor, he heard a loud crack.

"Hurry, Joe," Genji said urgently. "I can feel the floor giving way."

With one last quick tug, Joe pulled the broom and its passenger up to the step where he was crouched.

Genji scrambled onto the stone and huddled there for a few seconds. Her jeans were covered with dirt and splinters. A large spider slithered off her sneakers and back into the darkness.

"Get me out of here," she said with a shudder. She wiped off her clothes and shoes, then climbed the steps and crawled through the opening.

Joe joined Genji on the other side of the wall, and they pushed the loose boards against it.

Joe motioned for Genji to be quiet as they walked up the hall. Swiftly, they darted around the fish counter and blended back into the City Market crowd.

They walked back to the station and secured a food-court table just as Frank and Jackson wandered in. Over pizza, Joe and Genji told the others about their adventure at the City Market.

"So, what about you guys?" Joe asked. "You find out anything when you were at Silvio's?"

"There are definitely rooms under there," Frank said. "We talked to the cook and an old-timer who hangs out at the diner."

"Silvio's family has had some sort of restaurant there since the 1850s," Jackson added.

"No one knows for sure what the rooms were used for," Frank said, "but people think that Silvio's might have been a stop on the Underground Railroad."

"The Underground Railroad wasn't really a railroad, right?" Genji asked, passing the pizza.

"Right," Frank said. "There were no tracks or

trains or anything like that. It's just a term used to describe the network of people who offered hiding places that escaping slaves used as stopping points on their way north to freedom."

"What do the rooms below Silvio's look like?" Joe asked.

"Most of the rooms were all brick—brick walls, floors, and ceilings," Frank said. "Some had dirt or stone floors and stone ceilings. They're all connected with brick or stone halls."

"They'd be great for shops and clubs," Genji said, "the way Buonnarti has planned."

"Nobody's using them now," Frank said, taking a brownie. "They were bricked up during the 1920s."

When they had finished eating, Jackson said that he wanted to get his camcorder from the train car suite for some sightseeing. The four went through the heavy glass doors to the hotel side of the train shed. As they trooped down the hall toward the Barnum car, Frank gasped and grabbed his brother's arm.

"Look," Frank said, pointing.

The other three followed his gaze to the top of the train car next to theirs. There, across the top, were three large brass letters: J P S.

"So?" Joe said. "It's the John Philip Sousa car— you know, the band composer."

"Right!" Frank said, pulling a crumpled scrap of

57

paper out of his pocket. "Remember the cookie shop receipt on Sam Bellamy's dashboard? The handwritten note on the bottom: 'JPS, 7P—'"

"And today's date," Jackson jumped in. His voice was excited. " JPS—John Philip Sousa."

"What if Bellamy is going to meet someone at seven tonight?" Frank suggested. "Maybe JPS isn't *who* Sam is meeting, but *where.*"

"What time is it now?" Genji asked.

Jackson checked his watch. "It's six o'clock."

"Let's set up a stakeout," Joe said. "The JPS car is right next to ours."

They hurried into their train car. "We can use my camcorder," Jackson said. "I'll set it up."

"Great," Frank said. "If we see something suspicious, we'll have it recorded for evidence."

"I've got six two-hour tapes," Jackson said. "If we start recording at six-thirty, that should be plenty." He set up the camcorder on the table beneath the window in the bedroom. He positioned it between the slats of the blinds so that it was pointed at the steps leading into the JPS car.

They took their places. Joe and Genji pulled chairs up to the desk in front of the sitting-room window. They could see anyone passing by their train car and headed for the JPS. Jackson and Frank posted themselves at the camcorder.

Fifteen minutes went by with no activity in the

hall. Ten more minutes passed, then Jackson murmured, "Looks like you were right, old buddy."

Striding quickly toward the JPS train car suite was Lane Donovan. Frank checked his watch. It was five minutes before seven o'clock.

Donovan disappeared up the three steps onto the vestibule at the end of the JPS car. From their vantage points, none of the four investigators could see whether anyone greeted him.

"So, what do you think?" Joe asked his brother. "Is he meeting someone already in there? Or is someone else still coming?"

"Keep watching," Frank answered.

"Bingo," Joe said at seven-fifteen. Coming up the hall were Sam Bellamy and Hamilton Harte. They walked to the JPS train car suite and disappeared from view.

"Wait," Jackson said. "Bellamy's leaving." They all watched as the guard strolled back down past their suite and left through the food-court door.

A half-hour passed with no more activity. "Why would Donovan and his uncle meet here?" Genji wondered. "They could meet at their home."

"There must be someone in there already who they're meeting," Frank pointed out.

"You know," Genji said, "it could be just an innocent business meeting."

"Yes," Frank agreed, "but my instincts tell me it's something more."

"Maybe it's a ransom meeting with the model trains thief," Joe pointed out.

"Could be," Frank said.

"Looks like the meeting is over for one of them," Jackson interrupted. Donovan walked quickly down the hall toward the exit door.

"It's eight-thirty," Joe said.

"I hate to leave," Genji said, "but I have to. I told my father I'd be home by now." She called the hotel desk for a cab. "I'll call you tomorrow," she said as she left.

The Hardys and Jackson kept up the stakeout. At ten o'clock, Jackson said, "Donovan's back." They watched Donovan head up the steps to the JPS train car suite as Jackson kept the camcorder going.

"I'd sure like to be a fly on the wall in there," Frank said.

At ten-thirty, Jackson replaced the camcorder tape. Fifteen minutes later, Donovan left the JPS train car suite for the second time.

Hours passed. The Hardys and Jackson took shifts sleeping and watching.

At four-thirty A.M., Frank ended his shift and Joe took over. "Anything happening?" Joe asked.

"Nothing," Frank said. "Harte has never come out. I don't understand it. We saw him go in. He must be sleeping in there. But why would he?" Frank walked over to his bed and lay down.

Finally, the Hoosier State screeched into the

station next to the Hardys' train car. "Here comes the rolling alarm clock," Joe said, from his lookout spot at the desk. "It must be six-thirty."

Jackson stretched and yawned. He sat up on the couch where he'd been dozing. "Catch any more activity?" he asked Joe.

"Nope," Joe answered. "Nothing."

"You know what that means," Frank said, coming into the front area. "Harte's still in the JPS car."

They took turns washing up and changing, so that one of them was always on lookout duty. There still was no activity in the hallway.

Soon a hotel maid appeared, headed for the JPS car. She was pushing a large laundry cart.

"Come on," Joe said. "I have an idea." He bolted out of the car and down the steps. The others followed quickly behind.

"Hi," Joe said to the maid, his face beaming with a big smile. "Could we ask a favor?"

"Good morning," she responded. "Ask away."

"We've heard so much about the decorating in the John Philip Sousa car," Joe said, remembering the brochure description. "Could we just peek inside and see it?"

"People always want to see the Sousa car," she said, nodding. "Well, just a minute. Let me see if there's anyone inside." She walked up the steps and knocked on the JPS train car door. Joe followed closely behind her.

"It will be interesting to see what Harte says when he sees we're staying next door," Frank whispered to Jackson, "especially if this was supposed to be a secret meeting. Watch his reaction for clues."

The maid knocked again, then used her key. She peered inside, calling, "Housekeeping. Hello, it's housekeeping."

Finally, she turned to them and said, "Come on up. You can peek in for a minute. There's nobody here. The car is empty."

7 A Surprising Clue

Joe darted past the maid and through the car, peering inside the bedroom and opening the closet and bathroom doors.

"Empty!" Frank repeated, as he and Jackson scrambled up the steps and into the traincar.

"Hey!" the maid said. "I said you could look inside, not make a search. Okay now, that's enough. I've got cleaning to do."

Frustrated, the Hardys and Jackson looked around the room one last time. "Come on, Joe," Frank said. "He's not here."

They thanked the maid and went back down the steps to the hallway. With a sigh, the maid disappeared inside the uninhabited JPS car.

"I don't get it," Jackson said, scratching his head.

"When did Harte leave? And when did the mystery person—the one he was meeting—leave?"

"One of us must have dozed off while on shift," Joe said. "Hey, not me," he added, when Frank looked at him closely with his eyes narrowed.

"Chill out, Joe," Frank said, exasperated. "Who slept on shift isn't the problem right now. Let's stick with the real mystery: Why did Harte and Donovan meet in that train car suite last night? And who were they meeting?"

"And when did Harte and the other person leave?" added Joe. He and the others returned to their car.

"It's got to be on the tape," Frank said. "Even if one of us dozed off on shift, the camcorder just kept cranking."

"I say we scan through the tapes," Jackson said. "If we watch it on fast-forward, we should spot when Harte or anyone else might have left."

When the phone rang, Frank answered. It was Genji.

"Everybody up?" she asked.

"Sure," Frank said. "What's happening?"

"I have an invitation for all of you," Genji said. "My seventeenth birthday is tomorrow."

"Hey, congratulations," Frank said.

"Thanks," Genji said. "My father had planned a surprise party for me, but I wormed it out of him."

Genji giggled, then continued, "My friend Beth Moore has rounded up some of our Indy friends for a blast tonight. I hope you guys can come. I know it's short notice."

"Sure," Frank said. "Sounds great." He turned to his roommates. "Party tonight?" he asked his brother and Jackson. Both gave him an enthusiastic thumbs-up.

"We're on," he reported back to Genji.

"Now for the best part," she said. "Father has rented the Forest Dinner Train for the party."

"What's the Forest Dinner Train?" Frank asked.

"It sounds really cool," Genji answered. "It's an old steam train that has been fixed up. It takes off from Indy and winds around through the hills in the southern part of the state."

"Great!" Frank said. "Jackson will really love that—Joe and I will, too. Hey, anything new on your end about the model trains robbery?"

"No, not really," Genji answered. "My dad must've been out late last night, and he was gone before I got up this morning, so I haven't had a chance to ask him anything else. But I did hear that Buonnarti isn't pressing charges against Harte for destroying the mall model."

"Why not?" Frank asked.

"The Moores think that Buonnarti is the kind of guy who wants his prey out in the open where he can see him. What a jerk," she said. "Well, I'd better get off the phone. I've got lots of party details to plan."

"Okay," Frank said. "We'll see you later."

"'Bye," Genji said. "We're all meeting at the boarding platform—six-thirty. See you guys then."

"I heard about that train at the collectors' meeting," Jackson said when Frank repeated the party plans. "It has a restored Nickel Plate Road Iron Horse steam locomotive—a real antique."

"Genji says it actually goes somewhere," Frank said.

"Yep. It goes south into the Hoosier National Forest," Jackson said. "It'll be great."

After breakfast, Frank went to the City/County building, across the street from the market. He headed straight for the Department of Public Works to get information about underground Indy.

He talked briefly with the assistant superintendent of the department. She showed him a few photographs of rooms and hallways and identified them as the ones beneath Silvio's Diner.

"What about the Catacombs? Does that area connect to the rooms under Silvio's?" Frank asked.

"No," she answered. "They were two entirely separate areas—never connected."

"I know Mr. Buonnarti wants to use some of the underground in his new mall," Frank pointed out.

"Well, yes, he has mentioned that," the woman

said. "But he's talking about the rooms below Silvio's, and there's a lot of work to be done down there before his plan would be possible."

Frank thanked her for her time and headed back to the Station.

Meanwhile, Joe and Jackson had decided to find out more about the meeting in the John Philip Sousa car. They rehearsed their plan, then went down to the registration desk.

"Hello," Jackson said to the hotel clerk. "I would like to book the John Philip Sousa car for the weekend. Is it available?"

"Let me see," the young man said, checking the computer record. "Ah, no, sir, I'm sorry. That suite has been leased for this entire year."

"Wow," Joe said. "That's pretty cool—living in a train car for the whole year."

"It would be," the hotel clerk agreed, "but in this case, it's been leased by a company as a corporate hospitality suite."

"Some local company?" Jackson asked, trying to sound casual.

"I'm sorry, we cannot release that information," the hotel employee said, turning to answer the phone.

Joe poked Jackson gently in the ribs. "Keep him busy," Joe whispered, slowly stepping back.

Jackson leaned his arms on the high counter. "I thought perhaps if you would just tell me who is leasing it, I could talk them into renting it to me for one weekend for the party I have planned."

While his friend rambled on, Joe quietly stepped to the end of the counter so that he had a clear view of the computer screen behind the desk. He read the name of the company on the screen and his eyes widened.

Slowly, he rejoined Jackson, who was still keeping the desk clerk busy. "Well, come on, pal," Joe said, tapping Jackson's shoulder. He tried to keep his voice calm. "I guess you're out of luck this time."

"Thank you anyway," Jackson said to the clerk, smiling.

Joe led Jackson around to the lounge area. "You're not going to believe it!" he said. "The JPS car is leased to Agawa Industries, Limited!"

8 A Perilous Party

"Genji's father is leasing the JPS car?" Jackson said. "Wow!"

"Come on, let's get back to our suite," Joe said. "Frank will be back soon to look at last night's video with us." They quickly headed back to the Barnum car.

"We should be able to see on the video when Harte left," Jackson said. "Are we going to ask Genji if she knows that her father is leasing the JPS car?"

"What? Who?" Frank said. He came up behind them as Joe and Jackson climbed the steps to their traincar vestibule. "Agawa is leasing the JPS car?"

"'Fraid so," Joe said. He told Frank what he and Jackson had learned at the registration desk.

"Wow," Frank said, frowning. "That's a surprise."

"So are we going to tell her?" Joe asked.

"I don't think we should," Frank answered. "If she already knows and hasn't told us, then she doesn't want us to know for some reason."

"What reason could that be?" Jackson said.

"I don't know," Frank said, "but I don't want to tip our hand if that is the case."

"Yeah, and if she doesn't know, I don't want to be the one to tell her," Joe said. "That's her father's job."

"Right," Frank agreed.

The three friends hauled sandwiches and soda out of their refrigerator and settled in the sitting area. Joe phoned down to the hotel desk for a rental VCR.

While they waited, Frank told the other two what he'd learned at the Department of Public Works.

"It doesn't sound as if it's a done deal for Buonnarti to use the underground in his mall, does it?" Joe asked his brother.

"Sure doesn't," Frank agreed.

Just then there was a knock at the traincar door. It was the hotel bellboy carrying a videotape player. Frank tipped him and carried the VCR over to the desk.

"I've been thinking," Joe said. "Maybe Harte is right about the collection being stolen for ransom."

"What makes you think so?" Frank asked as he helped Jackson hook up the VCR.

"Maybe the thief is going to trade the trains for Harte's building," Joe said with a knowing smile.

"So he can get on with his mall plans!" Frank said with a grin.

"Hmmm," Jackson remarked, putting a cassette tape into the machine. "I hope so. I'd much rather Buonnarti's the culprit and not Genji's dad. I'd hate to see a fellow collector go to such extremes."

"Well, gather round, gang," Frank said. "Let's run them on fast-forward for now," he suggested. "If anyone sees anything, yell out and we'll make a note of the tape counter. Then we can go back and check each suspected spot in slow motion."

It took them an hour to run through the tapes in fast-forward. Each noticed a few spots where someone might have been approaching or leaving the traincar, but running those places in slow-motion revealed no sign of Harte.

"Nothing," Joe said, disappointed.

There were no signs whatsoever of Harte leaving the JPS traincar on any of the tapes. Frustrated, they finally gave up.

That evening, the Union Station boarding platform was full of laughing teenagers, excited about their excursion into the forest in honor of Genji's birthday.

71

Frank, Joe, and Jackson wove through the crowd, introducing themselves to the others. There were about twenty kids, most of them in their late teens.

While Frank was talking to Genji's host, Beth Moore, he noticed something out of the corner of his eye. Someone was lurking in the dark shadows behind an ornate column at the end of the platform.

Frank excused himself and made his way through the group of partygoers. He found his brother talking sports with a couple of guys.

"Come on, pal," Frank said softly to Joe. "There's someone or something over there. Let's check it out." The brothers walked quickly in the direction of the shadowy figure.

A man was hiding behind the column, and when he saw them coming, he bolted away. From that distance, the Hardys couldn't identify him.

The Hardys split up. Joe took off across South Street, Frank went down an alley.

It was very quiet in the alley. Frank eased up, slowing his pace so that his shoes wouldn't betray his presence. His eyes narrowed as he peered into the darkness, trying to find the shape of the man they had been following.

Frank felt his pulse pounding in his temples. He knew the stranger could be anywhere—in a doorway or behind the trash cans stacked at the far end.

Suddenly, a ferocious clanging stopped him cold.

The hair on the backs of his arms bristled against the yarn of his sweater.

A scrawny white dog bolted from behind the trash cans, knocking one over as he ran.

Frank took a deep breath as the dog scurried by him. Turning, Frank walked quickly back up the alley. "If the guy was here, he's gone now," he mumbled to himself, "thanks to all the commotion."

When he reached the street, he looked around for Joe's football jacket, but there was no sign of him. Frank heard the steam whistle of the dinner train as it approached the station, so he headed back toward the boarding platform.

Frank walked into the Station just ahead of the train. The locomotive was an awesome sight— massive, black iron, chugging and puffing huge balloons of white steam into the night air.

The steam whistle blew an old-fashioned and very loud harmony—a chord of three notes.

As Frank waved to Jackson in the crowd waiting for him up ahead, he felt a hard shove against his back. He lurched forward, stumbling toward the edge of the platform.

Behind him, he heard the wheezing iron giant plowing into the station.

Frank flailed his arms wildly in the air to try to regain his balance, but he couldn't. With a jolt of terror in the pit of his stomach, he plunged off the cement platform four feet to the tracks below.

The braking squeals of the locomotive filled his ears, and he could feel the tracks vibrating beneath him.

9 A Mysterious Disappearance

The old locomotive's brakes screeched as the train bore down. His heart pounding, Frank rolled once, jumped to his feet, and scrambled to safety on the adjacent set of tracks.

He raced to the steps leading to the opposite platform as the train wheezed past him to a stop. An agitated stationmaster was there to meet him. "Are you all right?" the stationmaster asked. "You had a terrible fall!"

"Yes, I'm fine," Frank said, not mentioning the shove he'd felt in his back.

The stationmaster escorted Frank down into the train bed and back to the boarding platform.

"Are you okay?" Joe asked. "Man, that was close." He brushed off his brother's sweater.

Jackson and Genji joined them, followed by several of the other kids. "Frank, what happened?" Genji asked. "Did you trip?"

"Not exactly," Frank said. "I'll tell you later. I'm okay."

Finally, the party climbed a three-step metal stool into the dinner train. The train had just three passenger cars. The first was furnished with blue-and-white lounge chairs and small tables.

Jackson led the group on a tour of the other two cars. The second car had a kitchenette. The refrigerators and cupboards overflowed with pizzas, fried chicken, salads, biscuits, fruit, juice, and sodas. A huge birthday cake rested on the counter.

The last car had rows of empty seats and a small private area at the end with facing seats and stools, a large supply closet, and two restrooms.

While the gang settled in the large, comfortable chairs in the first car, Jackson checked out the locomotive.

"You should see the setup," he told the Hardys when he returned. He put his glasses in a vest pocket and showed them the engineer's cap that the crew had given him. "It's just like the one I'm doing my training on back in Bayport." He was barely able to control his excitement. "There's a three-man crew—engineer and two firemen."

At that moment, one of the firemen came into the

car. "I'm doubling as your conductor," he announced. "Welcome aboard. If everyone is here now, we'll get started." He stepped off the train, checked the platform, waved to the engineer, and hoisted the metal stool aboard.

With a snort and a loud whistle, the Iron Horse lurched and chugged out of the station.

One of the partygoers had brought a boom box and an assortment of CDs. Others went into the kitchenette car and began warming pizzas and chicken in the microwaves. Soon the party was in full swing.

"Okay, give," Jackson said, as he, Joe, and Genji cornered Frank. "What happened back at the station?"

"Joe told us about that man you two followed," Genji said.

"I was *pushed* onto those tracks," Frank said grimly, remembering the horrible moment when he realized he was falling in front of the train.

"Do you think it was the same guy you were chasing?" Genji asked, her eyes wide.

"Could be," Frank said. "He could have given us the slip, then doubled back and waited."

"First the horse and carriage, now this. . . ." Jackson said. Joe and Frank exchanged looks. They both knew what these "accidents" meant.

"Someone doesn't like us," Joe said.

77

"Maybe someone wants us to stop snooping around," Frank said. "We seem to have attracted some attention with our investigation."

The gang partied for an hour and a half while the train followed the scenic White River Valley to the great hills of southern Indiana. The train chugged deep into the Hoosier National Forest.

"We're making a short stop at Forest Station," Jackson told the Hardys. He had just returned from another visit to the engine crew. "It's an unmanned facility, but the firemen punch a clock there."

Within minutes, the train began a long slowdown, but most of the kids didn't notice. They were intent on celebrating Genji's big day. By the time the train reached Forest Station, the partygoers were gathered around the counter in the kitchenette that held Genji's huge birthday cake.

During a loud rendition of "Happy Birthday," the Hardys and Jackson watched the two firemen leave the locomotive and walk the dark path to the small cabin next to the tracks.

"Blow out the candles," Jackson urged. Everyone began chanting and clapping. The seventeen flames were soon extinguished to resounding cheers. "Now open your presents," someone yelled. Grinning, Genji picked a gift from the stack.

Minutes passed, then half an hour. As the rest of the group laughed and cheered, Frank and Joe exchanged glances. Frank looked at his watch, and they both looked out the window at the small building. There was no one in sight.

"What's up?" Jackson said, joining the Hardys.

"How long do we stop here?" Joe asked.

"A few minutes," Jackson said. "Long enough for the crew to punch the clock and wash up."

They all looked out again, then at each other. "I'll check with the engineer," Jackson said. He was back in minutes. "No sign of him," he said, frowning. "I don't get it. They wouldn't all leave at the same time."

The Hardys and Jackson walked through the car and stepped onto the vestibule.

The last car was still empty. They checked the rest rooms, then Joe said, "Hey, wasn't this closet unlocked when we first boarded?"

"Yep," Frank said, joining him. "It had napkins, towels, cleaning supplies, stuff like that. One of the crewmen must have locked it."

"Hey guys," Genji's voice called behind them. "What's the deal? Why aren't you at my party?"

Joe went over to her, saying, "We're wondering why the crew hasn't returned. Jackson said they're just checking in—it shouldn't take this long."

Frank noticed a glint of alarm in Genji's eyes. "Hey, it's probably nothing," he quickly assured her. "Joe, why don't you and Genji go back to the party. They'll notice if the birthday girl is missing. Jackson and I'll go see what's going on."

Frank and Jackson got down from the rear of the last passenger car. It was very quiet in the forest. Only an occasional owl's hoot or coyote's wail penetrated the silence. Their footsteps crackled on dry pine needles as they approached the little cabin.

The door was open, and the light inside was on. A time clock was mounted on the wall next to a small table with a coffee maker on it.

"Look," Frank said, pointing to the machine. A paper cup brimming with steaming dark coffee sat on the warming stand, waiting for the person who had poured it.

"How about this?" Jackson pointed to the time clock. A card was stuck in the slot, waiting to be pushed down and punched.

Frank felt an eerie feeling at the back of his neck. Something was very wrong here.

He darted over to the rest room door and, in a quick movement, kicked it open and jumped back. The room was empty.

He tried the phone, but it was dead.

Frank and Jackson cautiously checked the ground around the building. "We've got trouble," Frank said, holding up the phone line. It was severed.

Great, he thought, realizing that the party was stranded in the middle of the massive hills and trees of the dark forest. As they walked back to the train, Frank saw Jackson shudder.

Joe met them when they reboarded. "Where've you been?" he asked in a low voice. "Genji and I tried to keep them from catching on, but they're starting to get a little restless."

Frank ushered Joe, Jackson, and Genji into the empty passenger car. "The crew's gone," Frank said as the door whooshed shut behind him. "I don't know where or how, but they've disappeared!"

Joe combed his fingers back through his blond hair. "Whoa," he said in a low voice. Genji covered her mouth with her hands and her eyes widened.

"I'm going back up to the engine," Jackson said. "There's a headset there. We can call somebody." He returned within minutes. "It's been yanked," he said. His expression was grim.

"Jackson, you're the closest we've got to an engineer. Do you think you can handle this train?" Frank asked.

"I can give it a try," Jackson said. "I might need both of you to help keep it going."

"Genji, you go back to the party," Frank said. "Tell the others as little as possible. We don't want anyone to panic. We'll get down from this car and reboard directly into the engine," Joe said.

"If anyone wants to know where we are, tell them about Jackson working on his apprentice certificate," Frank added. "Say he's picking up some instruction, and we're keeping him company."

"Are you sure this is a good idea?" Genji said. "Can't we wait for help? Or call someone?"

"No one knows we need help," Frank pointed out, "and the station's phone doesn't work." He decided not to tell her about the severed line or the pulled engine headset.

"We need to start back," Joe said, taking his brother's cue. He gently pushed Genji back into the kitchenette. "Do your best to keep the gang busy."

The Hardys and Jackson jumped off the car and ran through the dark to the front of the train. Quickly, they scrambled up into the cab of the Iron Horse. "Let's move," Frank said. "I don't know what happened to the crew, but I don't think we should wait until it happens to us."

The engine was enough like the one back home that Jackson managed to get it fired up after a few false starts. As he had been instructed back in Bayport, he clutched the brass lever that hung at a right angle from the ceiling of the cab.

"This lever controls the locomotive's airbrakes," he told the Hardys as the train began to move. "I need to hang on to it while the train is moving—we call it 'riding the brakes.' You guys stoke the fire."

He showed Frank and Joe a handle to turn that automatically released coal and wood into the firebox.

The moon was locked behind a thick cloudbank, adding to the creepy atmosphere of the dark woods.

The only lights they could see for miles around were the locomotive's lampbeam and occasional pairs of animal eyes glinting as they chugged by.

"According to this diagram, there's a huge hill ahead," Jackson said, pointing to the map on the wall next to his seat. "The tracks weave up and around the hill. Once we get to the other side, we'll be out of the forest."

"I'm sure we can get some help when we get back to civilization," Frank said.

Soon the tracks began climbing the steep incline. When they finally reached the top, Jackson pulled the air brake lever.

Suddenly, all the lights on the train went out. They could hear shouts from the passenger car. "What happened?" Joe yelled.

"I don't know," Jackson said. The locomotive stopped, then bumped forward again, then started down the hill.

Frank turned on a battery lantern swinging from a hook in the corner of the cab.

"I'll go check on the gang," Joe said.

"The lights are out in all the cars," Joe reported when he returned. "Nothing's working but the emergency lights at the end of each car."

"They're on batteries," Jackson said. "Each car has its own generator, so either all the regular lights failed at once—"

"Or someone helped them along," Joe said.

Then Frank noticed that Jackson was pulling the brake lever again and again. "Jackson, what is it?" Frank yelled. "What's wrong?"

"Forget the lights, guys," Jackson said, as sweat trickled down his face. "We've got bigger problems. This loco's brakes are out! If we don't get this baby under control, we'll fly right off the hill!"

10 A Wild Ride

Picking up speed as it started down the hill, the old locomotive swung perilously from side to side. Joe heard shouts turn to screams as the partygoers were thrown around in the cars.

The train raced faster and faster. Frank was thrown against the wall of the locomotive as the train careened down the hill.

Jackson reached up and pulled back on a head-high lever. "I've shut off the throttle," he said through gritted teeth. "That stops the steam." Then he turned to the Hardys. "Okay, let's slow this loco down."

Jackson showed Frank the controls for the feedwater pump. "We've got to get some water into the boiler to cool it off. You man the controls while I watch the pressure gauge."

Then he turned to Joe. "Stoke the fire," he said. "Fill the box as fast as you can. We need to smother the fire."

As the fire went out, smoke backed into the cab and the three began coughing. Within seconds, they were covered in black soot.

"So far, so good," Jackson said with a scratchy voice. "Now we have a chance if we can make it to level ground."

The loco still felt like a wild bull as it stormed and bounced down the hill. "Joe," Frank said, toweling soot off his brother. "Go tell the gang everything's going to be okay."

"Right," Joe said, "they're really going to believe that." He stumbled through the door and out onto the bouncing vestibule.

"If anyone can convince them, you can," Frank called after him.

Joe walked through the first passenger car. What a mess! Food was splattered against the walls, and soda cans rolled back and forth across the floor as the train lurched from side to side. Some of the group seemed to have enjoyed the wild ride, others wore expressions of pure terror.

"Joe!" Genji said, lurching toward him. The black night flew by the windows as the train continued its dive to the bottom of the hill. "What's happening?"

"I think we're okay," he told her. "Jackson knows a lot about these old engines. We'll get her under control." Silently, he hoped he was right.

"You stay here and tell everyone it's okay," Joe told Genji. "I want to check the rest of the cars."

He made a quick check of the kitchenette car. Total chaos. Food, napkins, ice cubes, and pizza boxes were everywhere.

Joe moved on into the last passenger car—the empty one. As soon as the door closed behind him, he felt his detective radar go up. He was not alone in this car.

Quietly, he crept along the aisle, holding on to the backs of the seats to keep his balance. His ears strained to hear over the rattling, clattering sound of the runaway train. The emergency lights cast an odd glow around the rows of seats.

When he reached the middle of the car, the door of the closet at the end of the car swung open, and a man jumped into the aisle, facing Joe. His head was covered with a black ski mask. Two dark brown eyes squinted out at Joe.

Before Joe could say or do anything, the man was on him. With one powerful lunge, the stranger's fist shot into Joe's stomach.

"Oooomph," Joe grunted. Stunned, he dropped to his knees as the man pushed around him and bolted toward the front door of the car.

Joe couldn't move for a minute. The wind was knocked out of him, and his gut ached. Finally, he got his breath, but by that time the man was gone.

Gathering all his strength, Joe headed toward the front of the train. He stumbled through the passenger car, gaining strength with every breath and every step.

Joe motioned to the others to keep quiet, but there was no need. The sight of the masked stranger had turned the crowd mute with shock.

Finally, Joe made it to the door. But before he could step through, the stranger's arm reached around, grabbed Joe's shirt, and hauled him out onto the wobbling vestibule between the first passenger car and the engine.

Joe wrestled with the man in the small space. "Who are you?" Joe asked through gritted teeth. "What are you doing on this train?"

The man said nothing, punching instead at Joe's face. Joe leaned back but was still caught with a few knuckles to his chin. He reached up to grab at the man's mask, but the stranger wriggled away.

Joe reached for him again. The stranger quickly moved to the door on the side of the vestibule, the door that opened to the outside.

Before Joe could catch him, the man hoisted himself out through the open half of the vestibule door and disappeared sideways outside the car.

Joe crept to the outside door. The wind roared as the train tore down the hill. The wheels clattered loudly against the tracks.

Joe saw a ladder fixed to the side of the traincar beside the door opening. "Well," Joe mumbled, "either he jumped into the hill or he took the ladder, and I'm betting on the ladder."

Joe reached his right arm around the outside of the car until he could grab a rung of the ladder. Then he reached his right leg over and planted it firmly on a lower rung.

Holding tightly with his right hand, he took a deep breath, then lifted the rest of his body over to the ladder. For a moment he hung on tightly as the train rounded a curve. His strong, muscular body didn't fail him.

He leaned in with all his strength, plastering himself to the side of the moving train. Carefully, he worked his way up the ladder. Each time he moved a hand or a foot the wind grabbed him, and he felt as if he were being pulled out into the black night.

When he was high enough, Joe peered over the top of the train. The stranger was standing up at the far end of the car, his back to Joe.

His heart pounding furiously, Joe hoisted himself up onto the roof of the train car. Lying on his stomach and holding the handrails located on the side of the roof, he inched along. His eyes never left the masked stranger ahead.

As Joe crawled, his confidence grew. First he got up on his knees. His body swayed in the wind, but he knew he had to do something.

Finally, he stood up. By this time, the man was two cars ahead of him, on the roof of the last passenger car.

Joe moved faster. When he got to the end of the car, he held his breath and jumped over the gap to the next car. He scrambled across the roof of the second car and jumped to the third car.

When he landed, the stranger wheeled around. Joe knew he had to act fast. There was no room for error on the roof of a speeding train.

The masked man made the first move—with his fist. The two exchanged a few off-balance punches. As they struck out at each other, they twisted and turned until Joe was facing the rear of the train.

Joe took a step forward and the man stepped back. Joe took another step. In the oval opening of the ski mask, the man's eyes opened wide.

In a flash, the stranger scrambled backward and lowered himself partway down the ladder on the side of the traincar. Before Joe could move, the man turned and launched himself off the rung.

He seemed to fly straight out for a moment, then dropped into the woods next to the tracks.

Still standing, Joe couldn't figure out what had happened. And then he felt it. Tickling the back of his neck, the soft ropes of a telltale brushed up and over his head. He remembered Jackson's words. Behind him, with no clearance, the train was heading into a tunnel!

11 Off the Track

When he felt the telltale rope brush his head, Joe knew that a tunnel was right behind him. He dropped to a prone position, grabbed the handrails, and held on with all his strength. The last thing he saw as he dropped was the stranger rolling to his feet and limping off into the dark night.

As the train barreled along, Joe watched the sides of the tunnel flash by. When the train emerged from the tunnel, he lifted his head. They were slowing down at last. Joe swung back down off the train roof and into the vestibule.

Cheers and whistles greeted him as he burst into the passenger car. "Thank heaven you're safe," Genji said, grasping his hand. "We saw that guy take off and we didn't know what had happened to you," she added.

"I'm okay," Joe assured her. "I'd better check in with the engine crew."

Frank and Jackson seemed to have the loco finally under control. They had reached flat land at last. "We'll be in Stone's Crossing soon," Frank told his brother, pointing to the diagram on the engine wall. "We're going to try to pull up there."

The Hardys weren't surprised to see a small army of police and train officials waiting at the Stone's Crossing station. More cheers roared out from the passenger car when Frank and Jackson brought the train to a stop near the depot.

All the partygoers piled off the train, eager to feel solid ground under their feet again. The Hardys, Jackson, and Genji headed straight for the group of officials.

"I'm Frank Hardy, this is my brother, Joe, and our friends Jackson Wyatt and Genji Agawa," Frank said, shaking hands with the man leading the group.

"Tru Hilliard, engineer supervisor for this line," one of the men said, shaking Frank's hand. "Who brought this loco out of the forest?"

Jackson stepped forward. "I did, sir. I'm a certified fireman and an apprentice steam engineer."

"We weren't trying to steal the train," Joe chimed in. "We were escaping. The crew disappeared at the Hoosier Forest station, and we had a nasty encounter with a masked man." He rubbed his sore arm. Soot clung to his jacket sleeve.

"We decided that we had better get out of there, and Jackson volunteered to give it a try," Frank said.

"With a runaway, we didn't know what to expect," Hilliard said. "You did a fine job."

"How did you find out about it?" Frank asked.

"When the train crew didn't check in at the Forest station, we called the Highway Patrol and asked them to check on it," Hilliard said. "Officer Haught called us," he concluded, motioning one of the patrolmen forward.

Officer Haught brushed his index finger against the bill of his uniform cap in a casual salute, saying, "We checked the Forest Station, but there was no sign of the crew."

"But where were they?" Joe jumped in. "We couldn't find them either." Briefly, the Hardys and Jackson told the story of their adventure, including the cut phone line, the pulled engine headset, and Joe's scuffle with the man in the mask.

"The police found them tied up and gagged in a locked maintenance shed a quarter-mile from the station house," Hilliard said. "The firemen had been waylaid in the cabin by your masked man and a buddy of his with a gun. He was masked, too."

"After they were tied up and gagged, the accomplice sneaked out to the train and used his weapon

94

to persuade the engineer to join the rest of the crew," Officer Haught added.

"The guy with the gun locked the crew in the shed," Hilliard said, "and the masked man left."

"To hide in the supply closet on the train," Joe said. "That's why it was locked when we went back there. He must have been in there already, just waiting to pop out."

"When we discovered we couldn't communicate with the engine," Officer Haught continued, "we tried to follow along with the train. But there are no roads along the track in the forest."

"By the time you got out of the hills," Hilliard added, "we could tell that whoever was engineering the train had some idea of what they were doing. We followed you along the highway."

Officer Haught turned to ask Joe, "So no one got a good look at the attacker's face?"

"That's correct, sir," Joe said, "but he may have hurt himself when he jumped off the train."

"Right," Genji added, joining the group. "He was limping when he escaped."

"Which leg?" the officer asked.

"Right," Genji said.

"Left," Joe said.

"It's pretty hard to limp with both, bro," Frank said.

"I think Joe's right," Genji said. "It was the left. After all, Joe, you're the detective."

"Excuse me," said Officer Haught. "The what?"

The Hardys briefly explained their background to the patrolman.

"You think this happened because of some case you're working on now?" Officer Haught asked.

The Hardys exchanged looks. "We're looking into some things around Indy," Frank hedged.

"Look, if you know something that would give someone a motive for endangering you all on this train, you know you have to tell me," the patrolman said. "Otherwise, you're withholding evidence."

"We don't at this point, sir," Frank said honestly.

"You guys are to be commended," Hilliard said. "You kept your heads and stayed cool. I hate to think what might have happened if you hadn't been aboard." He was interrupted by one of the inspectors, who mumbled a few words to him.

"Well," Hilliard said, "at least we know what happened to the loco's brakes. One of the reservoir nuts popped off. A team's left to look for it now."

The Hardys and Jackson smiled and shook hands with Supervisor Hilliard, then headed for the rest room to wash off some of the soot.

As they walked, Frank said, "You know, if we hadn't been on board, this might not have happened at all. I'm sure the masked man was trying to put us off the track."

"In more ways than one!" Joe said.

"Jackson, what's a reservoir nut and how does it pop off?" Frank asked.

"There's a main reservoir pipe that feeds air to the brakes. Large threaded nuts hold sections of the pipe together. If one of those gets loose, especially on a wild ride like ours, it can pop off, the pipe separates, and the loco's brakes fail."

"So the question is," Frank said, "was the loose nut an accident?"

At last the party reboarded the train for the short ride back to Indy. This leg was manned by an official crew, with Jackson watching and assisting.

Upon arriving safely at Union Station, the guests thanked Genji, some a bit more shakily than others. The Hardys and Jackson were debriefed again by the Indianapolis police, and Frank told them about the red-haired man who cropped up everywhere. A medic checked out Joe and pronounced him healthy but warned him to expect soreness and bruises.

The phone was ringing when they walked back into the P. T. Barnum car. It was Genji.

"Hi," Frank said. "What's up?"

"Well, I don't know," Genji replied. Frank could hear the nervousness in her voice. "It's my father. He's gone. I found out when I got home."

"Gone!" Frank said. "What do you mean?"

"Apparently, he and Harte have joined two other

97

collectors at a private meeting in Colorado," Genji said. "It was a last-minute deal—someone got hold of a transition pull train and invited a few select people to come see it."

"A transition pull train? What's that?" Frank asked.

"What's that!" Jackson echoed, jumping out of his chair. "Only one of the rarest antique toy trains there is. It's made out of wood and cast iron. It's got to be over a hundred years old."

Frank shushed him, saying to Genji, "You sound upset."

"Well, it's weird," she said. "He left me a note in the Moores' mailbox. He also said that he and Harte are going straight from Colorado to the convention next week. He's going to send for his clothes."

"The convention in Arizona?" Frank asked.

"Right," she answered. "The one for model train collectors."

"Jackson is headed there, too," Frank said.

"It's so odd," she said, the anxiety growing in her voice. "I mean, I know him. I'm not surprised he was willing to drop everything and go off to see this car or whatever."

Genji sighed and Frank could hear a catch in her voice. "But he didn't even stay to say goodbye or see us off on the dinner train. And tomorrow's my birthday. I can't believe that he couldn't wait a few hours and tell me in person. Plus he didn't leave any phone number or address where he's staying. There's no way I can get in touch with him if I had to. That's really not like him."

"Well, Genji, he knows you're in good hands with the Moores," Frank said, trying to ease her fears. "Maybe they had to catch a certain flight out and he couldn't wait. He'll probably call first thing tomorrow and give you more information."

"Maybe," Genji said. "It just doesn't seem right, somehow. Even the Moores think it was odd that he left so suddenly." Her voice trailed off.

"Look, we're all tired," Frank said reassuringly. "Let's sleep on it. Give us a call tomorrow when you get up, and we'll try to find out where they went—if he hasn't called by then."

"Okay, thanks." Genji yawned again, then mumbled, "'Night."

Frank hung up the phone. Quickly, he told the other two what Genji had said.

"She's right," Jackson agreed. "Any collector would drop everything to see a transition pull train."

"It does seem odd that Harte would jump and run like that, though, with his collection still missing," added Frank.

"I hate to say this," Joe began slowly, "but maybe I'm right about the collection being found."

Frank understood his brother's point immediately. "And this sudden trip is to go and get it," Frank said.

Jackson looked at the Hardys. "Agawa?" he said.

"It could explain why they disappeared together, and so mysteriously," Joe reasoned.

"I hope not," Jackson said. "He's one of the collectors I admire most."

"In any case," Frank pointed out, "there's no question that someone is trailing us and trying to throw us off the track."

"Yeah," Joe agreed, rubbing a bruised elbow. "But who?"

"Buonnarti," Jackson said. "That's my guess."

"Maybe," Frank said. "Turn on the VCR. I want to look at the stakeout tape again. Something's been bugging me all day."

"Uh-oh," Joe said. "Frank's detective button's been pushed." He checked his watch. "It's after midnight. Can't it wait till morning, big brother? I'm exhausted—and sore."

"Go take a hot shower," Frank said. "I'm just going to look at this for a few minutes."

Joe left and Jackson lay down on the sofa bed in the living area. Frank took the chair by the window and flipped on the first tape, fast-forwarding it to the point where Donovan left the JPS car.

Suddenly Frank yelled and paused the tape. Jackson sat up with a start. "What is it?" he asked.

"There," Frank said, pointing to the screen. "Look!" Lane Donovan was in the foreground, walking down the metal steps from the JPS car.

Behind him, coming around the back of the car was a man in a white maintenance uniform. He was pushing a large laundry cart. The man was wearing a hotel uniform hat instead of the Colts cap, but there was no mistaking that red hair!

12 The Underground Maze

Joe ran into the room from the bedroom. His blue terrycloth robe was damp, and he was toweling his hair dry. "What's the ruckus?" he said.

"Look at the screen. This is the beginning of the second tape, at eight-thirty the evening of the stakeout. Who do you see in the background?" Frank asked.

Joe moved closer to the TV, then whistled. "Well, if it isn't Mr. Redhead himself," he said.

Frank ejected the tape and popped the second one in. "And look at this. This would have been at ten forty-five," he said.

The red-haired stranger reappeared, pushing the laundry cart again.

"So he works for the hotel," Jackson said.

"Does he?" Joe asked. "Why is he following us? Maybe even sending wild horses after us?"

"Or setting up a runaway train?" Frank said. "You can hide a lot of red hair under a ski mask."

"Why would he be doing laundry at night?" Joe asked, easing his sore body down into a chair. "I thought the maid changes the linen."

"At eight-thirty *and* at quarter to eleven," Frank pointed out. "Twice in one night."

"I've got to sleep on this," Jackson mumbled. "I'm beat."

"You're right," Frank said. "We won't solve anything tonight. We'll get this tape to the police tomorrow. At least they'll have a picture of the man who's been following us."

The next morning, all three slept through the six-thirty arrival of the Hoosier State train for the first time since they'd arrived in Indy. At eight-twenty, the phone jangled Frank awake.

"Hi," Genji said. "I have incredible news. Are you up?"

"Not quite," Frank answered. He could hear Jackson showering, but Joe still slept soundly.

"Well, get moving," Genji said. "I'll be there in half an hour. You're not going to believe this."

Before Frank could say another word, Genji hung up. He jostled his brother gently, not wanting to add to the bruises Joe had from the scuffle on the train roof the night before.

By the time the three were up, showered, and dressed, Genji was knocking on their traincar door. "You're invited to breakfast," she said. "You don't need to bring anything. We're not going far."

Genji led Jackson and Joe down the metal steps to the hall while Frank locked the door. When he joined them, she said, "Okay, gang, follow me."

The three watched her walk down the hall and up the steps to the next vestibule. She turned the key in the door and disappeared into the John Philip Sousa traincar.

Joe galloped after her in spite of his sore muscles. The other two were close behind.

"Isn't this a kick?" Genji said. "I found a birth-day card from my father." Her arms swept around the red, white, and blue sitting room as she spoke. "He leased this car! Can you believe it? He's opening a research plant here and plans to use this car to entertain clients."

Genji plunked down onto the desk chair. "So I'm moving in," she said with a final flourish. "I'll be closer to the action on the case."

"Where was the birthday card?" Frank asked.

Genji's embarrassed blush matched her pink jumpsuit. "Don't tell, okay? After I talked to you last night, I couldn't sleep. I was concerned about

104

Father, so I snooped through his things. I thought I might find out where he is."

"Did you?" Joe asked.

"No," Genji answered, "but I found my birthday card in the bottom of his shirt drawer. I guess he was planning on giving me my present when he got back. So I decided to open it and here I am. Okay, what do you want from room service?" she asked.

Frank could tell Genji didn't want to talk about her father anymore. In fact, she seemed close to tears. "I've got a better idea," he said. "I'll go over to Silvio's and pick up breakfast."

"Fine," Genji said. "I have to blow my nose," she added, heading for the bathroom.

"Hey guys," Frank said before he stepped out the door, "she's really upset about her dad."

"What do you think?" Joe asked. He kept his voice low. "Has he blown town, or has something happened to him?"

"Leaving town the way he did, especially on her birthday, looks pretty suspicious," Frank said as he left. "See what you can find out, but go easy on her."

When Genji returned, she said, "Tell me something, you guys."

"Sure, Genji, anything," Joe said.

"You don't seem to be as bowled over with my news as I'd thought. In fact, it's like you already knew that my father had leased this car."

105

Joe and Jackson exchanged looks. "Well . . ." Joe began, his mouth drawn tight.

"You did know!" the girl said. "But I don't understand. Why didn't you tell me?"

Joe started to speak, but before he could, Genji wheeled around and looked at him. "You think my father is involved somehow in the model trains robbery? Is that it?"

"Genji," Jackson said, pulling his vest on over a blue-striped shirt, "we didn't say that."

"You didn't have to," she answered. "It's written all over your faces."

"Good detectives weigh all the possibilities, Genji," Joe said, "and keep their minds open."

"What about me?" she said, obviously distressed. "Do you think I had something to do with the robbery?"

"Of course not," Jackson reassured her. "Genji, no one has said your dad is guilty of anything, either."

Joe gave the girl a warm smile. "Actually," he said, "we figured that if your dad hadn't told you about this car, it wasn't our place to do it."

"And we were right," Jackson said. "It was supposed to be a birthday surprise. You wouldn't have wanted us to blow that, would you?"

"No, I guess not," Genji said.

"Now, do you mind if we look around a little?" Joe asked Genji.

"Not at all," she answered. "I'll help. What are we looking for?"

"Anything that shouldn't be here," Joe said. He pushed up the sleeves of his blue sweatshirt.

The three went to work on the traincar, searching every corner. They lifted mattresses and pillows and checked behind the refrigerator. "By the way," Joe said, "did your father mention the surprise trip to Colorado on the birthday card?"

"No," Genji said, reaching behind the bathroom sink. "He must have written the card before the Colorado trip came up."

"Were both notes handwritten?" Joe asked.

"The one on the card was," she answered. "The other was a computer printout. Probably from his notebook computer. He never travels without it."

Joe fished out a small crumpled paper wedged between the headboard of one of the beds and the wall. As he unfolded it, Frank burst into the room, shouting, "Great news! *Really* great!"

"What is it, man?" Joe said, smoothing the scrap of paper.

Frank carried the takeout bags with breakfast over to the table and put them down. He was grinning from ear to ear.

"There *is* access to the underground rooms below the diner, fellow detectives," he said, rubbing his hands together. "And yours truly has talked the owner into letting us down there."

107

"No lie?" Jackson whooped. "Terrific!"

Joe came over and gave his brother a high five. "Good going, Frank. How'd you manage it?"

"Well, we talked for a while, and I just wore him down," Frank said. "Actually, Silvio said he'd opened the underground for someone else several times this week, so he might as well for us."

"Who's the someone else?" Genji asked.

"He wouldn't tell me," Frank said.

"Buonnarti, I bet," Joe suggested.

"Could be," Frank agreed. "He wants the underground for his mall. And Harte went nuts when Buonnarti told him that, remember? Something about the underground has fueled their feud."

Jackson and Genji grabbed a cardboard container and a cup of juice and joined Frank at the table. The food was hot, delicious, and Italian: eggs with pepperoni and cheese, potatoes with onions and bell peppers, toast made with thick Italian bread, and a variety of luscious pastries.

They wolfed down the food, babbling excitedly about the underground. "Wait a minute," Jackson said. "Joe, what was on the paper you found?"

"I wondered if any of you would remember," the younger Hardy said with a secretive smile. He smoothed out the paper again and read, " 'Must see you regarding funds we discussed—urgent.' It's signed," he said, pausing for effect, " 'L.D.' "

"Lane Donovan," Jackson said.

108

"Yes, but who's it to?" Joe said. "Harte?"

"Or my father?" Genji said, her voice a whisper.

"What about the thief?" Frank said. "Maybe Donovan is talking about ransom money."

"Why would a thief contact Donovan and not Harte?" Genji asked.

"Maybe he's working as Harte's agent," Frank said, "a go-between. You said he's sort of his uncle's shield."

"Well, I say let's move out," Joe said.

"Give me a minute to get some junk," Frank said. He went back to the Barnum traincar. Looking around the room, he thought about what they might need. Then he grabbed his backpack and packed it with his cellular phone, flashlight, compass, and city map.

Genji, Jackson, and Joe were out in the hall waiting for him when he came out. "All set?" Jackson asked, popping a last bit of pastry into his mouth.

"Set!" Frank said with a grin. The gang headed out.

It was a few minutes up Market Street to the diner. Silvio took them through his kitchen and downstairs to a low, narrow door in the corner of his cellar. He unlocked it and urged them to be careful.

The four scrambled eagerly through the door. Frank led the way with the powerful flashlight from his backpack.

Cautiously, they walked down a dozen steep stone steps to the underground.

The room directly below Silvio's was large— about as large as the diner. From there, hallways with high ceilings led to dozens of rooms with brick walls, stone floors, and wooden doors.

Most of the halls were empty. Occasionally, they came across a tool or a pile of rubble. A chisel and a small wooden sledgehammer leaned in the corner of one room.

The main hallway forked and branched into several smaller ones. "Boy," Joe exclaimed, "this sure is a maze."

Each hall had several rooms off of it. The group opened wooden doors and inspected each room. They found nothing but piles of bricks or planks of wood and hundreds of cobwebs.

They passed under one spot in the main hall where they could see some sort of trapdoor in the ceiling. A few more twists and turns in the spooky passageways and they came to an odd door. Unlike the other doors, it was not an old wooden one. A rusty axe leaned against the wall beside it.

The door wasn't new, but it wasn't from the last century, either. It was made of steel, and had no knob or handle. Frank and Joe held their ears up to it, but they could hear nothing from the other side. So the group kept going.

Finally, they came to a dead end. The hallway just stopped at a brick wall.

Reluctantly, they started back. After a few wrong turns and some backtracking, they found the main hall and set out for the room under Silvio's.

Frank still led the way with the flashlight. Joe was right behind him with the map, and Jackson and Genji walked side by side behind the brothers.

Without warning, one of the wooden doors crashed open, smashing into Frank and knocking him and the flashlight to the ground!

13 Going Down?

Frank lay gasping for breath. Joe scrambled for the flashlight and swung it around.

Captured in the light was the stocky body of Hamilton Harte's rival in yellow coveralls. Vincent Buonnarti's face was dark with anger as he reached down toward Frank.

"Why you—" Joe yelled. He tossed the flashlight toward Genji. She caught it and kept the beam steady as Joe tackled Buonnarti.

Joe grabbed the big man's legs and pulled them out from under him. Buonnarti's voice echoed around the honeycomb of underground halls and rooms when he bellowed at Joe. They both went down with a thud.

"Joe!" Frank said, his voice low but firm. "It's okay." Jackson pried the two apart.

Buonnarti reached into the room he had come from and brought out a battery-operated construction lamp and turned it on. It cast a powerful light that brought the whole hallway into clear view.

"Wait a minute," Buonnarti said, moving closer. "I've seen you before. First you were at the demolition, then at the unveiling of my mall model."

"That was a public unveiling," Frank said quickly. "We were there to—"

"Oh no," Buonnarti thundered. The lamp cast a huge shadow of him against the rosy brick wall. "You weren't there as part of the public," he sneered. "You're involved with Harte somehow. You're all getting out of here right now, if I have to drag you out one at a time."

He took a menacing step forward, but Frank put up his hands. "Mr. Buonnarti," he said. "You've got it all wrong. We don't work for Mr. Harte."

"We're students," Joe chimed in.

"History buffs," Jackson added, nodding.

"Foreign exchange," Genji piped up, smiling.

"Right," Frank said. "We're just visiting Indy and heard about the legend of these rooms being used as part of the Underground Railroad."

"Silvio told us about it," Joe said, "and I talked him into letting us look around down here."

"This place will be wonderful," Genji said. "Are you going to have shops down here or restaurants?"

"Well, uh, I thought maybe a few clubs,"

Buonnarti said, softening, "and some boutiques."
Warming to his subject, the developer led them
around the maze.

When they passed under the large trapdoor in
the ceiling of the main hall, Joe stopped. "Where
are we now, Mr. Buonnarti?" he asked. "What's
above that trapdoor?"

"Union Station," Buonnarti said. "We're directly
beneath the hotel laundry room."

"I'm wondering, Mr. Buonnarti, what if the underground isn't available," Frank said cautiously. "I
believe I read that it isn't a done deal yet."

Buonnarti wheeled around, his eyes narrowing
into tiny slits in the lamp's eerie glow. "Oh, it's
gonna happen," he said. "In spite of Mr. Harte."

In front of them, Frank noticed the odd un-
marked steel door with no handle or knob that the
Hardys and their friends had seen when they first
started through the underground.

"Where does that door lead?" Frank asked.

The developer seemed to become agitated.
"Enough," he growled between clenched teeth.
"Get out. You don't belong down here."

"Take it easy, we're going," Frank said, startled
by the sudden change in the man. Quickly, the four
detectives raced back toward the diner. Frank
paused for just a moment to pick up something
shiny from the dirt floor.

114

"That guy's a real loose cannon," Joe said as they emerged into Silvio's.

The four sat at a table to catch their breath, and Jackson ordered a round of sodas. "Did you recognize that steel door we saw?" Frank asked the others. "It looks like another one we've seen recently." He tipped the glass to his mouth and took a long drink.

"Whoa," Joe said, slapping his forehead with the palm of his hand. "Harte!"

"That's right, bro," Frank said. He turned to Jackson and Genji, who both looked puzzled.

"Think back to Harte's display room," Frank said. "It had three doors—the main door, the workshop door, and a third one." He paused while they pictured the scene, then said, "It was metal with no knob or handle, like the one below."

"There's got to be a way to get to that room from *inside* Harte's building," Frank said. "Let's grab lunch, then head on over there."

They ate quickly, eager to go to Harte's and search for clues. It was a five-minute walk to Harte's. On the way, they hatched a scheme.

"It looks like Sam Bellamy's here," Frank said. "Okay gang, let's do it."

"What brings you all here again?" Bellamy asked, greeting them at the gate.

"Hi, Mr. Bellamy," Frank said. "We'll get to that

in a minute, but first, we had some questions and thought if anyone could help us out, you could."

Bellamy tilted his head. "Is that so?" he said. He sounded as if he didn't quite trust Frank.

"Did you take Mr. Harte and Mr. Agawa to the airport for their trip to Colorado?" Frank asked.

"No," Bellamy said. "Mr. Donovan did."

"Did you see Mr. Harte yesterday?" Frank asked.

"As a matter of fact, I didn't," Bellamy answered. "I was out of town."

"Really?" Frank said. "So the last time you saw him was when you escorted him to Union Station the night before last?"

"Right," Bellamy said. "I took him over and— say, what is this?" Bellamy's eyes narrowed as he scanned the group. "Some kind of third degree?"

"Not at all," Frank said. He spoke quietly and slowly, so his voice wouldn't be threatening.

"Well, how did you know we were at the station?" Bellamy asked.

"We saw you there, that's all," Frank said. "We're staying there, too. Boy, that's some hotel."

"Why did you take Mr. Harte?" Joe asked. "Why didn't he go by himself? Or with Mr. Donovan?"

"I wanted to see the Sousa train car," Bellamy said. "Mr. Donovan wasn't there, was he? I didn't see him." He seemed surprised by that piece of news. "Anyway, I left after I got a good look."

116

"So Mr. Harte and my father must have worked up their trip to Colorado that night," Genji said.

"How did you find out about their trip, Mr. Bellamy?" Joe asked.

"Mr. Donovan left a message about it on my phone machine," the guard said.

"Were you surprised that Mr. Harte didn't contact you personally?" Frank asked.

"No," Bellamy said. "I wasn't in, remember? And Mr. Harte usually has Mr. Donovan make his calls."

"You were out of town yesterday?" Joe said, smiling. "Maybe went down to the track? We saw your picture in the paper. You're a celebrity, man."

Bellamy seemed to relax a little. "Yeah?" he said. "Do you really think so?"

"Sure," Jackson chimed in. "You have pretty good luck at the track?"

"Some good, some bad," Bellamy said, then chuckled. "A whole lot better than some I could mention."

"Anyone we might know?" Joe asked.

"Sure," Bellamy said. Then his smile disappeared. "Hey. I still get the idea I'm being grilled. You never told me what you're doing here."

"Oh, right," Frank said innocently. "As you know, Jackson here is also a renowned collector."

"And a close personal friend of Mr. Harte," Joe put in, motioning Jackson forward.

117

"Hamilton called me last night," Jackson said, taking a deep breath. "He left in such a hurry that he forgot some model parts and a special tool. Hamilton and Mr. Agawa are going straight to the model train collectors' convention next week, so he asked me to pick up the items from his workshop and bring them to him there."

"Hmm," Bellamy said, looking at the group.

Jackson took a step closer to the fence and spoke in a stern voice. "Hamilton said you would let us in. If I arrive at the convention next week without the things he has requested, he will be very angry. We don't want that, do we?"

Bellamy paused a moment longer, then finally reached up to trip the gate lock. "Okay," he said, walking toward Harte's building. "After all, there's nothing valuable left to steal." He unlocked the door, tripped the electronic security system, and opened the display-room door.

"It may take hours to find what I need," Jackson warned the guard, heading for the workshop.

"No matter," Bellamy said. "I'll hang around." He sat on a stool in the corner of the workshop.

Jackson turned so that his back was to Bellamy. With a wink, he said to the others, "Everyone grab a box. We're looking for three-inch curved Code 70 rail. If you find a piece of curved rail, bring it to me and I'll check to see if it's Code 70."

The Hardys, Genji, and Jackson each took a box

and sat at one of the worktables. Carefully, they picked each broken part out of their boxes. Once in a while, Genji, Joe, or Frank would find a small piece of curved rail and take it to Jackson. "Nope," he would say each time. "That's not it."

Frank watched Bellamy grow bored and impatient. He checked his watch three times during the first half-hour. Finally, Bellamy said, "You guys seem to be doing okay here. I'm going back to my place."

"We'll check back with you when we leave," Frank assured him.

The four waited until Bellamy was out of sight. "Let's get to work. There's the door I mentioned— the one that's like the door in the underground," Frank said.

"You guys really had Bellamy going when you were questioning him," Genji said with admiration. "Do you still think he might have had something to do with the theft?"

"I don't know," Frank said, running his hands down the side of the metal door. "He sure could have been an accomplice. We know he lied about what he was doing part of the day of the theft."

"Remember the night we discovered the theft?" Frank asked. "Mr. Harte hustled us all out into the hall and locked the door behind us."

"Sure," Genji said.

"Think back to what we heard," Frank said.

"The whistling?" Joe asked.

"Yes!" Frank said. "Mr. Harte used the silver whistle to start the train display, right?"

Everyone nodded and waited for him to continue. "Well, I read that someone at Harvard had once rigged up a voice-activated computer to respond to a pattern of sounds," Frank said, "the same way Mr. Harte did with his train set."

"I have a friend in Japan who is paralyzed," Genji said, "but she starts and stops her wheelchair, TV, stereo, and computer with a whistle.

"I still don't get it," Jackson said. "Why was he whistling *after* the trains were stolen?"

"There must be something else that's activated by a whistle pattern," Joe said, looking around.

"And look what I found in the underground," Frank said, pulling a shiny whistle from his pocket.

"Harte's whistle!" Joe cried. "Way to go! That means Harte has been down there."

Frank nodded, saying, "Watch that door." He whistled a pattern of notes that he thought was the pattern Harte had blown. Nothing happened.

"Frank, I think you have one note wrong," Genji said. "Try this." She hummed a few notes.

Frank tried it, and with a soft swish, the heavy door swung open!

"Wow!" Joe said. "You did it!" Behind the door was a tiny but fully equipped computer room. Joe and Genji stepped inside the small room.

The computer screen showed that a program was loaded and ready to go. In the center of the screen was one question: DO YOU WISH TO DESCEND? PRESS Y FOR YES, N FOR NO.

Impulsively, Genji reached toward the computer.

"Genji, no!" Joe said. "Wait till we check—"

It was too late. Genji pressed the Y key.

It was very quiet except for an answering beep from the computer. Then a new sound started up—a low, humming sound.

Joe checked the computer screen. The words OKAY, YOU ASKED FOR IT! flashed across the center. The room seemed to shudder as the new sound echoed around the empty circular room like an eerie moan.

Frank and Jackson felt a sudden jolt and their knees buckled. Frank leaned the palm of his hand against the wall to help him regain his balance. "Uh-oh," he said, as the wall slithered upward under his palm. "Hang on, Jackson," he cried. "We're going down!"

14 A Grim Discovery

"Frank!" Joe yelled. Helpless, he watched as Frank and Jackson began descending on the floor of the circular room.

"Okay!" Joe yelled. "Wait for me." Joe jumped down onto the lowering floor.

Genji watched the computer. "There's a new message," she said. "It reads, 'Do you wish to ascend? Press *Y* for Yes, *N* for No.'"

"You'd better stay up there," Frank said. "That may be our only way up."

"Whew, this is really great," Joe said. "Just like a haunted-house ride."

"This must be why Harte gets so angry when Buonnarti talks about using the underground in his mall," Jackson said.

"Right!" Frank agreed. "We're taking Harte's

private elevator to the underground. He must have set up this trick floor as extra security."

"I'll bet the crook used this for the theft," Joe said. He looked around as the floor finally stopped twenty feet down. "Unless, of course, Harte used it himself to squirrel the trains away."

"Then where are they?" Jackson asked. The floor stopped at the bottom. They looked around, but there was nothing to see—just a twenty-foot-high wall and the door leading to the underground.

They heard a strange whoosh above them. Looking up, they saw another round floor moving across to fill in the space above.

"Look," Frank said. "He even rigged it so that another floor would fill in. It must be stored in a pocket under the workshop room."

"But why?" Jackson asked. "I don't get it."

"If he felt that the collection was threatened," Frank explained, "he could go to the computer room, send the collection into the underground, then fill in with the new floor."

"It would look like a normal room," Joe said.

"Except without the collection," Jackson said, his eyes wide.

"Which would be safe and sound, all closed up from anyone's sight down here," Frank concluded.

"Wow! It's like a huge safe," Joe said.

"There's the door we saw from the other side," Frank said.

"Maybe the whistle opens this one, too," Joe said. "Try it."

Frank blew the whistle code. Nothing happened.

"Okay, Genji, bring us up," Joe yelled. The false floor above pulled back and returned into hiding in its pocket beneath the workshop room. Then the floor that the Hardys and Jackson were on slowly began its ascent.

The four spent the next hour exploring Harte's workshop. "Uh-oh," Genji said, pulling something from a workbench drawer.

"What is it?" Joe asked, hurrying to her side.

"It's a note from my father to Mr. Harte," she said. "I feel funny reading it."

"I'll read it, if you'd prefer," Joe offered.

"No," she said. "I will. If I think it's important to the case, I'll share it with all of you."

She read silently for a few minutes, then said, "You guys, this is definitely something. Listen."

The letter said that Donovan had contacted Genji's father for a large loan, and Agawa thought Harte ought to know about it.

"That ties in with the meeting in the JPS traincar suite," Joe said.

"Yes," Genji agreed. "Maybe Donovan came there to meet with Father about the loan."

"But we never saw your dad," Jackson said.

"And it doesn't explain what Harte was doing

there," Frank said, "unless it was to discourage his nephew from taking money from Agawa."

"So what's next?" Jackson said. "We've pretty much taken this place apart."

"Frank, if the trains were taken down on the floor elevator," Joe asked, "where are they now?"

"Maybe they're still there somewhere," Frank said.

"So, let's go," Joe said. "I'm ready."

"Wait a minute," Frank said. "Let's think this through. Someone should stay here."

"I want to try to locate my father in Colorado. I still don't understand why he left so suddenly," Genji said. "I'm afraid something's wrong."

Frank and Joe exchanged looks. The case was heating up, and they knew Genji may have something to worry about. Finding the note seemed to rattle her. Was her father a victim? Or a criminal?

"Okay, let's do this," Frank suggested. "Genji, you go back to the JPS car and call some of your father's collector friends. See if you can find out where he and Harte went for this private meeting."

"I know several people I can call," she said.

"Good," Frank said. Then he turned to Jackson. "You're the obvious one to leave here. It will make the most sense to Bellamy because you're the collector, doing a favor for Harte."

"I can handle the computer," Jackson agreed.

"Bro," Frank said, turning to Joe, "you and I will go back to the underground.

"I brought the phone," Frank added, patting his backpack. "We'll call you, Jackson. Maybe we can figure out how to connect this room to the rest of the underground."

Frank, Joe, and Genji left Jackson and stopped by Sam Bellamy's bungalow. As they'd expected, the guard saw no problem with Jackson staying in the workshop.

Within minutes, the Hardys were headed back through Silvio's kitchen and into the Indy underground. They went over every room and hallway. Nothing had changed since they were there before.

They came to the metal door that led to the space below Harte's building. Joe looked around, and his voice was low when he spoke. "Hey, big brother, is it my imagination, or does this space seem spookier now?"

"It is creepy down here," Frank said with a shudder. "I wish we had Buonnarti's lamp."

"Yeah," Joe said, "as long as we don't have to have the man himself—and his temper."

Frank tried the whistle a few times, but the door wouldn't open. Then he phoned Jackson in Harte's computer room. "Send it down," he said.

The Hardys leaned against the door. They heard the hum of the elevator floor. They tried the whistle

126

a few more times, and Jackson tried from inside. But they still couldn't open the door.

"Well, that's it for now," Frank told Jackson over the portable phone. "At least we're sure that this door does lead into the space below Harte's."

"If you don't need me here anymore, I'm going to get the floor back up and head out," Jackson said. "Maybe I can help Genji figure out where Harte and Agawa have gone. I've thought of a few collectors she might not know about."

"Great," Frank said. "We'll hang out here for a while, see if we can dig up anything more on the trains. We'll meet you back at the hotel when we're finished."

The Hardys heard Harte's trick floor go back up, then they turned and headed along the last underground hallway. It curved to the same dead end they had reached earlier—a brick wall.

Frustrated, they started back. As they passed a small room, Joe picked up a piece of broken brick and threw it into the room with all his strength. It bounced off the far wall with a hollow echo.

Startled, the brothers looked at each other. "Did you hear that?" Frank asked.

Joe answered him by racing to the wall where he'd thrown the brick. "You know," Joe said, "I read once that the rooms used for the Underground Railroad often had false walls that opened into more secret hiding places."

Frank placed the flashlight so that it threw a beam onto the wall. The two began tapping the wall with rocks, listening for the hollow sound.

Finally, they found a spot that sounded different. They concentrated their efforts, hammering and poking at the bricks, until—with a grinding creak —part of the wall gave way and swung open.

Frank flashed the light into the opening beyond the wall. He could see another brick room, smaller than the one they were in. He stepped into it, flashing the light around.

"Joe, come here!" he said breathlessly.

Joe stepped through the opening into the little chamber. Frank flashed the light toward a huge opening in the far wall. "It's a tunnel!" Joe said.

"A new one," Frank said, reaching to pull a handful of soil from a large pile in the corner. "This is fresh dirt."

The Hardys walked side by side through the long dirt tunnel, their heads nearly touching the ceiling. The tunnel was pretty much a straight shoot, curving only once before opening into a huge, musty-smelling room. At one end of the room hung a few plaques, banners, and targets, full of holes.

Stacks of new wooden crates and cardboard barrels lined one long wall. "Frank!" Joe said, his eyes wide. "I know where we are. This is the pistol range under the City Market. We're in the Catacombs! Genji fell through the floor down in that far corner."

"These are the rooms that are not supposed to connect with the underground beneath Silvio's," Frank said, nodding. "Looks as if someone has dug a tunnel recently for just that purpose."

"Maybe so they could store these new barrels," Joe said. He rushed to one of the barrels and pried up the lid. There, carelessly packed in shredded paper, was Harte's model circus train. "Frank, you're not going to believe this," Joe gasped.

"Help," whispered a voice from the end of the piled boxes. "Please, help us."

Frank's stomach churned at the sound of the frightened voice. He and Joe ran to pull some of the boxes away.

"Oh no!" Joe said, his heart dropping to the pit of his stomach. Harte and Agawa sat against the wall, on the cold dirt floor. They were tied together with heavy rope.

"Mr. Agawa! Mr. Harte!" Frank exclaimed. "Are you all right?"

"My nephew," Harte said weakly. "Lane. He did this to us. He's a madman. He came to borrow money from Yoshio and I surprised him there. We had a furious argument, and he just seemed to snap."

"We've been here since then," Agawa added.

"We haven't eaten for over twenty-four hours, and our heads ache. They knocked us out."

As Frank and Joe untied the two men, they heard a noise behind them. Someone was coming through the tunnel toward the room!

Frank and Joe looked around. There was no place in the large room to hide. They crouched down near the two older men, behind the pile of boxes, and turned off the flashlight.

From their vantage point, Frank watched Donovan and the red-haired man burst into the room. The light of the portable worklamp in Donovan's hand showed that his accomplice carried a revolver!

15 A Pressing Danger

From behind the pile of crates and barrels, the Hardys watched the two men enter the room. They headed straight for Harte and Agawa.

"What the—" Lane Donovan said when he saw the Hardys. "Well, look at this. You were right," he said to his accomplice. "I can't say I'm all that surprised." He put down the worklamp.

The red-haired man wore the familiar Colts cap. He pulled Joe to his feet. Then he grabbed Frank's arm roughly and pulled him up and out from behind the boxes.

Donovan untied the rope that bound Harte and Agawa together and pulled them to their feet. Harte seemed a little weak, and he leaned against one of the crates.

"So you found us out," Donovan said. "I knew

you two were getting close to the truth." He gestured toward his henchman, saying, "My associate and I tried to discourage you several times, but you just wouldn't give up."

Donovan tied Frank's hands behind his back, then Joe's.

"The last time we were down here, it looked as if someone besides that fool Buonnarti had been prowling around," Donovan said. "My buddy here followed you into Silvio's, saw you go to the kitchen, and put two and two together."

Donovan picked up the work lamp, and the two men pushed Harte, Agawa, and the Hardys across the room. "So this time we used your route and sneaked down through the diner ourselves. And we were right," he concluded with a nasty smile. "Here you are."

"Donovan's limping," Joe whispered to Frank as they stumbled through the tunnel. "From jumping off the dinner train, I'll bet."

"Hey!" the red-haired man snarled. "Quiet."

Donovan and his accomplice pushed their captives back through the tunnel, through the little room's false wall, and into the underground hallways. The beam from the worklamp bounced around the brick walls in a crazy pattern.

When they reached the metal door leading to the room below Harte's building, Donovan put down the work lamp, pulled out a small cassette recorder and pushed the PLAY button. The tinny sound of a recorded whistle pierced the silence. The metal door opened.

"You found out about my special elevator floor," Harte said to Donovan. He seemed very tired and sad.

Frank thought that Harte's distress was caused as much by being betrayed by his own nephew as it was by the predicament they were all in.

"Yes, I did, dear uncle," Donovan said, sneering at the man. "I found the original construction plans for this building months ago."

Donovan pushed Frank, Joe, and Agawa into the room. The henchman followed, dragging Harte. Then he retrieved the work lamp and put it down so that it lit the scene with a spooky glow.

"I overheard your whistle codes one day," Donovan explained. "I borrowed the whistle when you were asleep and had the sounds duplicated digitally by a computer hacker friend."

The two criminals pushed their four captives onto the floor and tied them more securely. The red-haired man cut the straps on Frank's backpack with a pocket knife and kicked it over to the wall.

"Why are you doing this, Lane?" Harte asked. "We've had problems, but I never expected this."

"Look," Donovan said in a harsh voice, "I've got a lot of nasty characters coming down hard on me for my losses at the track. I'm tired of begging you for a few thousand here and there, and I can't wait for you to kick off to get it all. I'm afraid I'll just have to give nature a little assistance."

Then he walked over to tighten the ropes around his uncle's wrists. "Hey, this is your fault," Donovan said. "I was content with stealing the collection. I figured I could sell a few pieces privately whenever I needed some extra bucks."

He stooped to help his accomplice secure Agawa's ropes. "Of course, I knew I couldn't flash any of the collection around until the heat about the theft eased a little," Donovan continued. "I thought hitting up your rich buddy Agawa-san for a healthy bundle would keep the hit man off my back for a while."

Frank and Joe watched Donovan lean back on his heels. His expression was dark and menacing as he glared at his uncle.

"But you had to butt in, didn't you," Donovan said. "Well, you're going to pay for that now."

"You can't get away with it, Donovan," Frank said. "Our friends know where we are. We'll be free in no time."

"By the time anyone finds you, it will be too late," Donovan said. "I want these especially tight for you, my friend," Donovan said, pulling the ropes around Joe's ankles. "To pay you back for all the trouble you caused me on that train."

"I thought I noticed you limping," Joe said.

"Yes, I was on that train," Donovan said. "Agawa had told me about reserving it for Genji's birthday party. I did a little advance work and learned about the crew's routine."

Donovan rolled his uncle over onto his back. "My friend here and I drove down ahead of time, waited for the crew to check in, and disposed of them, and then I hid in the train's supply closet."

"Why would you want to come back onto a sabotaged train?" Frank asked. "You did monkey with the brakes, didn't you? It was a pretty hairy ride."

"I never really expected you to start her up," Donovan said. "I had planned some surprises in order to scare you and your friends until you were rescued—blowing the lights and yanking the engine headset were two of them. I wanted you to understand that you had better stop snooping around."

The red-haired man shoved Agawa and the Hardys roughly over onto their backs as Donovan had done with Harte.

"When I overheard you say you were going to start up the engine, I loosened the nut on the airbrake reservoir pipe. But when I tried to get off, you caught me." He glared at Joe.

"And now we have caught you," he concluded.

135

"I'm sorry, but you have forced our hand. We'll leave you the light so you won't miss any of the show." With that, he and his accomplice returned to the underground hallway, slamming the thick steel door behind them.

It was suddenly quiet. The only sound was the shallow, frightened breathing of fellow captives.

Frank and Joe began working with the ropes, using all their energy to try to get free.

They twisted their hands and feet, but the bonds held them tightly. Fifteen minutes passed while the Hardys struggled in frustration.

"Wait a minute," Frank said. "I just remembered something. Hold on." He twisted and rolled until the leather strap and whistle swung out from under his shirt. "Mr. Harte, what's the pattern to open the door?"

"You found my whistle!" Harte said. "Thank goodness." He hummed the code to unlock the metal door. Frank followed his instructions and, after one miss, blew the correct pattern. The heavy door opened.

Suddenly, Frank's heart skipped a beat. He heard a familiar humming sound. "Joe, we've got big trouble. Look."

His brother followed his gaze up toward the ceiling. "Oh no!" Joe yelled. "He wouldn't!"

The hum grew louder and louder. "My room!"

Harte yelled. "Good grief! He's dropping the elevator room."

The four captives looked up in horror as the floor of Harte's building—the ceiling of this large underground room—began lowering toward them!

16 Full Speed Ahead

"Come on!" Frank yelled to Joe as he began inching toward the open door.

With their arms still tied tightly behind their backs, the Hardys dragged themselves out of the room to the old axe, still leaning up against the wall in the hallway.

"I can't move," Harte said, his voice low.

"I think I can make it," Agawa said.

"Hang on, Mr. Harte," Frank said, watching the ceiling descend. He and Joe took turns sawing their ropes against the axe's rusty blade.

"Hurry!" Agawa said. "The ceiling's getting closer." He wriggled slowly to the door.

Frank looked back into the room. The ceiling was about ten feet above the two collectors. "Harder," he urged his brother. "Push into the blade. We've got to get free!"

"I'm slashing as hard as I can," Joe said. "I want to cut the ropes, not slit my wrists."

The ceiling continued its descent: nine and a half feet . . . nine feet . . .

At last Frank felt the ropes around his wrists break free. He crawled quickly back into the room, hobbled with tied ankles. He grabbed Agawa's shoulders and began pulling him toward the door.

He could hear the humming motor louder now. The ceiling was just six feet above his head.

Frank dragged the bound body of Genji's father, rolling him across the floor to safety out in the hall of the underground.

"Get Harte!" Frank cried. "Quick!"

Frank and Joe lay on their stomachs and crawled back in to get Harte. They each hooked an elbow under one of his armpits. Using their free hands and elbows, they started the long crawl back to safety.

It was like swimming in molasses. The door seemed so far away. They had to keep their heads down because the ceiling had lowered even farther.

"Faster!" Joe said. "We haven't got much time left. In a few seconds we'll be pancakes!"

With one last gasp, Joe and Frank pulled Harte through the door to the hallway. Frank reached his arm back in and whipped out his backpack just as the ceiling hit the floor. They could hear the crashing squeal as the work lamp was squashed.

Frank and Joe cut the rest of the ropes, and they all gulped in air. Even though it was damp and dusty, it was great to be breathing at all.

"Thank you, thank you," Agawa said. "I don't know what we would have done without you."

"To think that my own nephew would do such a thing," Harte said through gritted teeth. "Come on, let's get him and his ugly friend."

"Whoa, Mr. Harte," Joe said, putting his hand on the older man's arm. "Take it easy."

"We'll get 'em," Frank said. He pulled the flash-light and phone from his backpack and called 911 for police and paramedics to come to Silvio's. Then he called Jackson in the JPS car.

"They'll be here shortly," he said. "Genji is very happy that you're okay, Mr. Agawa." He didn't mention that she was also relieved to find out he was not a crook.

"Mr. Harte, do you think you can walk to Silvio's?" Joe asked. "We can have the medics come down here if you'd rather."

"Nonsense," Harte said, rising carefully to his feet with Agawa's help. "Lead on. I'm with you."

They walked slowly through the halls, led by the beam of Frank's flashlight.

"Mr. Harte, I hate to bother you with this now, but I need to ask you a few questions," Frank said.

"Sure, my boy," Harte said. "After what you've done, you may ask anything you like."

"When you realized the trains were stolen, did you come down here and see if they were in the underground?" Frank asked.

"Yes," Harte replied. "That was my first guess. But I couldn't find them anywhere. I didn't know about the secret room and the tunnel to the Catacombs until Lane dragged us back through them."

"What about Bellamy?" Joe asked. "Was he in on it?"

Mr. Harte sighed. "My guard Sam Bellamy—he used to be more dependable, but the last several years, he's been pretty worthless. He's not a thief, though."

"Why did you keep him on then, Hamilton?" Agawa asked.

"His love of gambling became very useful," Harte said, rubbing the knot on his head.

"It was Sam who told you about your nephew's gambling debts?" Frank prompted.

"Yes," Harte said, nodding. "He was the one who first tipped me off to Lane's gambling addiction, so I kept Sam on as an informant. It was because of Sam's reports that I had recently decided that my nephew could no longer be trusted."

"That's an understatement," Joe said, expertly guiding the two older men through the hallways of the underground.

141

"Hmmph," Hamilton grunted. "Apparently so. He has become so twisted he was clearly prepared to kill us all to save his own skin."

By this time, the four had almost reached the room below the diner. "But what happened that pushed him into the kidnapping?" Frank persisted.

"Lane apparently had run into serious trouble with some bookmakers," Harte said. "When Yoshio told me Lane had asked him for money, I had to do something."

"Hamilton and I set up the meeting with Lane in my train car," Yoshio explained. "Lane arrived first, thinking he was going to get the loan. Then Hamilton surprised him, and we both tried to talk to him about his gambling problem."

"He wouldn't listen," Harte said, stopping to sit for a moment on the steps leading up to Silvio's. Frank and Joe heard sirens above.

"Lane excused himself to make a phone call," Harte continued, "and soon that ugly partner of his showed up."

"They knocked us both out," Agawa said. "When we woke up, we were in the room where you found us."

"We videotaped the hall beside your traincar that evening," Frank said to Agawa.

"We didn't know it was yours at the time," Joe explained, "but we saw a note in Bellamy's car that indicated a meeting was taking place there."

"We think your nephew and his accomplice took you out of the train car one by one in a laundry cart," Frank continued.

"Yours is the last car in the row, next to the wall," Joe concluded. "That late at night, taking you out at the far end of the car—there's a good chance no one would have seen them. We noticed a trapdoor in the ceiling of one of the halls down here. They might have brought you down that way."

"Father! Oh, Father!" Genji's voice rang through the musty air as she and Jackson rushed down the stone steps from Silvio's cellar.

"Hey, Hardys," Jackson said, slapping high fives with them. "Can't wait to hear the details."

As the group climbed the stairs to Silvio's, Frank took one last look around the underground. For a moment, he thought he could hear ghostly voices of past visitors to this strange place. Then he followed his friends on up the steps, his arms and legs tired and aching.

The paramedics pronounced the Hardys fine and found nothing really wrong with Agawa because of his general good health. They prescribed soup and juice right away and rest for the next twenty-four hours.

Harte was taken to the hospital for overnight observation. The Hardys wished him well, and he said he would be in touch.

As the ambulance door closed, they heard Harte say, "My trains. Don't forget my trains."

"I have taken care of it," Agawa said with a bow. He turned to face Joe and Frank. "I just called a private security firm," he told them. "We must keep the entrance to the underground secure until Hamilton's collection is safely removed."

Agawa looked around. "Who is the owner here?" he asked. Frank introduced him to Silvio. As he left them, he overheard Agawa making a generous offer to Silvio for the inconvenience of having Agawa's private security on guard there.

While the police questioned the Hardys, Jackson, and the Agawas, a call came from another officer to say that Donovan had been captured at the home he shared with his uncle. He'd been found packing for the collectors' convention in Arizona.

"He confessed," the officer at Silvio's told the Hardys. "Cracked like a rotten egg."

"He was going to the convention?" Genji said.

"Probably because that would be a great place to find someone with no scruples who might be interested in buying a treasure or two," Frank said. "No questions asked."

"It seems that Donovan originally planned the heist for next week while his uncle was out of town," the officer reported. "But he owed big bucks to some serious criminals and they gave him until tomorrow to pay up or his gambling—and his breathing—days would be over.

"You knew about the damage at his place the night of the Kreek Building demolition?" the officer continued.

"We were there when it happened," Joe said.

"Well, his uncle stayed up all night to fix one of those gizmos," the officer said, "and when he finally got home, the nephew slipped him a mickey to knock him out. Then he had his accomplice call Sam and invite him to an irresistible crap game. That left the collection free and clear."

"Still seems pretty risky," Jackson said.

"Not as risky as dodging gambling debts to a couple of Chicago heavyweights," the officer pointed out. "You pick your priorities."

The Hardys, Jackson, and the Agawas told the police all that they could remember. They explained that they would be leaving Indy the next day but gave them forwarding information and promised to contact them if they could think of anything else.

"We've put out an APB on the red-haired bum," the officer said before he left Silvio's. "He doesn't work at the hotel. He's a real sleaze, a racetrack buddy of Donovan."

Their duty done and the excitement over, everyone left the diner. Everyone, that is, except Mr.

Silvio and Mr. Agawa, who sat down to large bowls of the soup of the day.

The Hardys, Jackson, and Genji were given a lift in a squad car back to the hotel. More starving than exhausted, they stopped at the food court for one last meal together.

"I don't understand something about Harte's trick elevator floor," Genji said as she reached for a burger from the stack Jackson had bought. "Why were there no controls at the bottom when the floor was lowered? Wouldn't there be a chance he could get stuck down there?"

"That's what we were talking about when Joe and I walked with him from the underground," Frank said. "I asked him that same question."

"It wasn't an elevator for people," Joe explained. "He never went down on that floor. It was an elevator for the collection that he lowered and raised from the computer room upstairs."

Joe reached for a second burger. "It really was like a hidden safe," he said. "If he ever thought the trains were in danger, he could activate the floor and they would be safely hidden away."

"People walking into the room after the second floor filled in wouldn't detect a thing," Jackson added.

"Had he ever used it for real?" Frank asked.

"No," Jackson said. "Until this week, it was just another toy to play with."

146

"But then why did he have the door down there?" Genji asked.

"The door into the underground was a backup that he hoped he'd never have to use," Joe said.

"In case something happened to the electronics or computer that manipulated the trick floor," Frank said, "he could always go down and bring out the collection through that door. He knew about the underground, of course, and knew that if he had to, he could somehow get the trains out that way."

"Amazing," Genji said. "This has been just about the most exciting week of my life."

"And it's not over yet," Joe said. "Look there, big brother. Do you see what I see?"

Hurrying through the food court with his back to them was Donovan's accomplice. "Genji, call station security," Frank said. "Use the red emergency phone on the wall. Come on, guys."

The man was no match for Joe, Frank, and Jackson. They surprised him as he opened the door leading into the hotel. Joe and Frank held him while Jackson disarmed him. From that point on, he behaved like the whining weasel he really was.

Two station security officers were there in seconds and dispersed the crowd that had gathered. Frank and Joe explained the day's earlier events to the officers. Then the Hardys, Jackson, and Genji accompanied the officers and the criminal to the station holding cell to wait for the city police.

"Lane Donovan has been arrested and even confessed," Frank told the red-haired man. "You're cooked."

"Hey, it wasn't my idea," the man, who said his name was Earl, whined. "It was all Donovan."

"How did you get Mr. Agawa and Mr. Harte into the underground?" Joe asked.

"There's a trapdoor," Earl answered.

"We knew that's how they did it," Frank said to Joe with a grin.

"It opens to an old hydraulic freight elevator in the hotel laundry room," Earl confessed. "I did some day work when they restored this place back in the eighties. I figured out how to make the trapdoor elevator work when Donovan approached me with his plot."

"You used the laundry cart to remove them from the traincar?" Joe said.

"And that's how you got all those crates and barrels down there, too, right?" Frank said.

"Yeah." Earl slumped down onto the floor.

The city police arrived quickly. "Well, you boys are sure keeping us hopping today." It was the same detective who had interrogated them at Silvio's. "Thanks again. You're off-duty now, okay?" He shook their hands once more, and he and his partner led Earl off to join Donovan.

Frank, Joe, Jackson, and Genji pushed through the heavy glass doors to the hotel and the hallway leading to their traincar suites.

"Donovan should have stayed on track and stuck to his original plan to steal the collection next week," Genji said. "He was really stupid."

"What do you mean?" Jackson said.

Genji smiled at her new friends. "Because if he were smart, he'd never have tried to pull it off with the Hardy boys in town!"

NANCY DREW® MYSTERY STORIES By Carolyn Keene

☐

☐ #57: THE TRIPLE HOAX	69153-8/$3.99	
☐ #58: THE FLYING SAUCER MYSTERY	72320-0/$3.99	
☐ #62: THE KACHINA DOLL MYSTERY	67220-7/$3.99	
☐ #63: THE TWIN DILEMMA	67301-7/$3.99	
☐ #67: THE SINISTER OMEN	73938-7/$3.50	
☐ #68: THE ELUSIVE HEIRESS	62478-4/$3.99	
☐ #70: THE BROKEN ANCHOR	74228-0/$3.50	
☐ #72: THE HAUNTED CAROUSEL	66227-9/$3.99	
☐ #73: ENEMY MATCH	64283-9/$3.50	
☐ #76: THE ESKIMO'S SECRET	73003-7/$3.50	
☐ #77: THE BLUEBEARD ROOM	66857-9/$3.50	
☐ #78: THE PHANTOM OF VENICE	73422-9/$3.50	
☐ #79: THE DOUBLE HORROR OF FENLEY PLACE	64387-8/$3.99	
☐ #80: THE CASE OF THE DISAPPEARING DIAMONDS	64896-9/$3.99	
☐ #81: MARDI GRAS MYSTERY	64961-2/$3.99	
☐ #82: THE CLUE IN THE CAMERA	64962-0/$3.99	
☐ #83: THE CASE OF THE VANISHING VEIL	63313-5/$3.99	
☐ #84: THE JOKER'S REVENGE	63414-3/$3.99	
☐ #85: THE SECRET OF SHADY GLEN	63416-X/$3.99	
☐ #86: THE MYSTERY OF MISTY CANYON	63417-8/$3.99	
☐ #87: THE CASE OF THE RISING STAR	66312-7/$3.99	
☐ #88: THE SEARCH FOR CINDY AUSTIN	66313-5/$3.50	
☐ #89: THE CASE OF THE DISAPPEARING DEEJAY	66314-3/$3.99	
☐ #90: THE PUZZLE AT PINEVIEW SCHOOL	66315-1/$3.99	
☐ #91: THE GIRL WHO COULDN'T REMEMBER	66316-X/$3.99	
☐ #92: THE GHOST OF CRAVEN COVE	66317-8/$3.99	
☐ #93: THE CASE OF THE SAFECRACKER'S SECRET	66318-6/$3.99	
☐ #94: THE PICTURE-PERFECT MYSTERY	66319-4/$3.99	
☐ #96: THE CASE OF THE PHOTO FINISH	69281-X/$3.99	

☐ #97: THE MYSTERY AT MAGNOLIA MANSION	69282-8/$3.99	
☐ #98: THE HAUNTING OF HORSE ISAND	69284-4/$3.99	
#99: THE SECRET AT SEVEN ROCKS	69285-2/$3.99	
☐ #101: THE MYSTERY OF THE MISSING MILLIONAIRES	69287-9/$3.99	
☐ #102: THE SECRET IN THE DARK	69279-8/$3.99	
☐ #103: THE STRANGER IN THE SHADOWS	73049-5/$3.99	
☐ #104: THE MYSTERY OF THE JADE TIGER	73050-9/$3.99	
☐ #105: THE CLUE IN THE ANTIQUE TRUNK	73051-7/$3.99	
☐ #107: THE LEGEND OF MINER'S CREEK	73053-3/$3.99	
☐ #109: THE MYSTERY OF THE MASKED RIDER	73055-X/$3.99	
☐ #110: THE NUTCRACKER BALLET MYSTERY	73056-8/$3.99	
☐ #111: THE SECRET AT SOLAIRE	79297-0/$3.99	
☐ #112: CRIME IN THE QUEEN'S COURT	79298-9/$3.99	
☐ #113: THE SECRET LOST AT SEA	79299-7/$3.99	
☐ #114: THE SEARCH FOR THE SILVER PERSIAN	79300-4/$3.99	
#115: THE SUSPECT IN THE SMOKE	79301-2/$3.99	
☐ #116: THE CASE OF THE TWIN TEDDY BEARS	79302-0/$3.99	
☐ #117: MYSTERY ON THE MENU	79303-9/$3.99	
#118: TROUBLE AT LAKE TAHOE	79304-7/$3.99	
#119: THE MYSTERY OF THE MISSING MASCOT	87202-8/$3.99	
☐ #120: THE CASE OF THE FLOATING CRIME	87203-6/$3.99	
☐ #121: THE FORTUNE-TELLER'S SECRET	87204-4/$3.99	
☐ #122: THE MESSAGE IN THE HAUNTED MANSION	87205-2/$3.99	
☐ #123: THE CLUE ON THE SILVER SCREEN	87206-0/$3.99	
☐ NANCY DREW GHOST STORIES - #1	69132-5/$3.99	

LOOK FOR AN EXCITING NEW

NANCY DREW MYSTERY

COMING FROM

MINSTREL® BOOKS
